An Affectionate DECEPTION

Other Novels by Kimberly Loper

THE HAUTEVILLE HEARTS

Iron Arm

THE FLOWERS OF LONDON

A Harmless Flirtation

The Flowers of London Series

BOOK 2

KIMBERLY LOPER

This is a work of fiction. Names, characters, places, and incidents either are the product of the author's imagination or are used fictitiously. Any resemblance to actual persons, living or dead, events, or locales is entirely coincidental.

ISBN: 978-1-951908-04-1

Cover art by Germancreative

Published by Romachic Publishing

www.kimberlyloper.com

Chapter 1

Like all frauds, Abigail Newell was not as she appeared. The eye of the beholder being what it was, only the surface mattered, and on the surface Abigail was all she ought to be. Her hair was pinned up in a customary style donned by nobility and her dress was in the latest fashion, doubtless having been acquired through some underhanded dealings in the alley behind some London haberdashery. Forcing a demure expression, as was most proper for a young lady of marriageable age, Abigail became someone new. A casual observer would never suspect her of being anything but what she most wished to be—an average, run-of-the-mill societal miss.

Unfortunately, at least in Abigail's experience, wishes rarely came true. Life would never be that accommodating. Instead, she would be precisely who her father told her to be, as had long been the expectation for her.

Taking a deep, fortifying breath, she alighted from the carriage which had conveyed her from the coaching inn of Freemont Glenn to Lady Eliza Bedford's residence of Edgemont in Shropshire. She knew from the lady's letters that the estate must be quite large. Even so, Abigail was unprepared for precisely how grand it would appear upon her first arrival.

Abigail's heart beat faster as she raised her eyes from the ground. The stairs leading to the front doors were full of servants waiting to greet her as if she were herself a grand lady. Suddenly feeling tiny and unequal to the task before her, she turned slightly, fighting the urge to return to the carriage. Then her eyes lit upon a familiar and friendly face.

"Dear Abigail," Lady Bedford said, her arms outstretched in greeting. She stepped forward and grasped Abigail's hands in her own. "I am so pleased you were able to come." Lady Bedford smiled warmly. She had taken to using Abigail's Christian name shortly upon making her acquaintance, a liberty Abigail felt unequal to denying the woman.

"You are looking well, my lady," Abigail offered.

"Eliza, please. We need not be so formal, particularly when speaking alone."

The last time Abigail had heard from Lady Bedford, the latter would have been shrouded in the black of deepest mourning. The account of her father's passing had been included in one of her earliest letters to Abigail, who could not understand the type of grief described within. She had often pondered what would become of her if her own father were no longer breathing, and mourned the end of each fantasy rather than the subject of such.

Abigail forced her concentration back on the character she was meant to portray.

Pleasant and demure. It was the same image she had portrayed while in London last year. She had attempted to escape her father, yet he had found her out and in response he had landed her in Harmony Hospital in the heart of London. Lady Bedford had frequently volunteered at said hospital, and had run across Abigail recovering from her injuries.

Placing a reciprocating smile upon her face, she answered, "I was happy to receive your generous invitation, my la-, I mean, Eliza. Though I am sorry to have put your servants out. There is no need for such a reception solely on my account." Her elocution was flawless, her unnumbered hours of privately practicing paying off as not one servant eyed her with suspicion.

"Nonsense, my dear." Lady Bedford guided her up the stairs leading to the grand front entry. "Although, I must apologize for my husband's absence. He is currently in London on some business, although we expect him shortly." She turned and addressed her butler. "Ridley, see that Miss Newell's trunks are taken to her room."

A man, sharply dressed in the Bedford livery, stepped forward and bowed. "Yes, my lady." He signaled to two footmen who immediately stepped down and began unfastening the straps holding the trunks to the carriage.

Lady Bedford pulled Abigail forward, ushering her into the house. "Come, we will get you settled. You are likely worn out after your journey, and I must visit the nursery. Little Phillip is perfectly cared for by his nurse, yet I find I need to see him more often than not to ease my own mind. I wonder if all new mothers struggle with the separation as I do." Seeming to notice Abigail's discomfort with such a topic, she added, "You need not concern yourself, dear Abigail. He shall likely remain in the nursery through the whole of your visit and is not likely to disturb you. Now, I will leave you to rest. There will be ample time for us to visit later."

Shortly after Lady Bedford's exit came a soft knock on the door and a maid entered.

"My name is Molly, miss," she said with a smile. "I will be helping you during your stay."

Having not anticipated having a servant at her disposal, Abigail wondered if she ought to refuse the proffered help. Her father had sent her with a bit of pin money which she could use to compensate the poor girl for her assistance. On the other hand, it would be interesting to be pampered for what time she could. Deciding it would raise questions should she refuse the proffered help, she allowed the girl to unpack her trunk and freshen up her hair. It all felt heavenly to Abigail, who was accustomed to doing everything on her own, as her father found such things to be beneath his dignity.

Abigail soon found herself left alone. She sighed in relief that the first part of her task was complete. Lady Bedford seemed to have no idea of Abigail's true purpose. It was no wonder, as Abigail prided herself in her ability to play a part. She had been playing one with her father for years. In fact, she could not think of a time when she had felt able to be her complete self with that man anywhere near her.

Laying upon the bed, she closed her eyes in a valiant attempt to rest before dinner. Instead of a peaceful repose, however, she clutched her stomach as dread for what she must do settled over her. She took deep breaths, and began counting in the hopes of getting her mind on something else. It was not long before she admitted defeat and rose. In lieu of lounging about unproductively, a quick self-guided tour of the house seemed appropriate.

She slipped out of her room, foregoing a search of the chambers on this level as they were all likely to be guest rooms and largely, if not entirely, unoccupied. Lady Bedford had made no mention of other guests, although that did not entirely rule out the possibility. If Abigail was to find out that there were indeed more guests, she would scour these rooms later.

Heart racing, Abigail paused at the top of the stairs to listen for signs of activity below before slipping down. She was not exactly doing anything wrong, yet, it was simply good to know what sort of situation one was getting into. Glancing in the first door on this level she passed by the music room. Having no accomplishments with instruments she would have no reason to explore there at present, although she might return later to take stock of anything valuable that could be quickly and surreptitiously removed.

Across the hall was an entrance into a grand ballroom. She took a few steps inside, and let her mind wander. Her imagination took over, and soon she envisioned herself dancing with Colin, her childhood friend. Thoughts of him often beset her even now, although many years had passed since their last meeting. Soon her vision changed to memory, and she was once more a girl of fifteen.

"Dance with me?" Colin asked.

Ignoring his proffered hand, Abigail laughed at his absurdity as she sifted the coarse sand through her fingers, remaining firmly seated on the beach. "You cannot be serious. There is no music."

"I will make our music," he insisted, seeming to miss the humor in the situation and being altogether too serious.

Her head tilted as she smirked at him. "I have heard you sing. It is not at all pleasant."

"Dance with me?" he asked once more, apparently not hindered by her slight. Looking out at the sea, he responded, "The waves will be our music."

Knowing Colin, he would not give up until he got what he wanted. But why would he wish to dance with her? The boy defied all understanding, as she assumed all boys must, although her experience with any others was severely limited.

"No," she answered flatly.

Colin knelt next to her in the sand. Taking her hand gingerly in his, he asked once more, his inexperience coming through with his hesitancy. "Dance with me?"

Gazing into those eyes that appeared black in the darkness of the night, she was touched by his sincerity. A rare trait among boys of any age, or so she supposed. As always, she wished to please him, yet as she was unable, she had to admit to her shortcoming. "I cannot, Colin. I do not know how."

Colin smiled, as if he had known all along, and gave her hand a gentle tug. "I will show you. Trust me."

Giving in, she allowed him to pull her to her feet, then she brushed the sand from her dress. Standing close to him proved how much he had grown over the past year while away at school. Being two years her senior, he had forever been taller, and now he fairly towered over her. Where at home she felt small and insignificant, next to Colin she felt sheltered and protected. This feeling was unique to her encounters with him.

Pulling her near, he showed her where to place her hands for the beginning of the set. He then took up his position to her left. Slowly, he guided her through the steps. Backward and forward, side to side, they moved in unison, each in their various patterns, none of it truly making sense to Abigail. Her trust in him had never failed and she allowed him to guide her along. Finally, she began to remember the complicated movements and as Colin no longer needed to instruct her, he began to sing as he had earlier threatened. Abigail was absurdly pleased with herself, until Colin's hand pressed on her back to guide her along one section, causing her to cry out in agony.

Immediately they stopped moving and Colin was all concern. "What is it?"

"It's nothing. I am sorry." Even as she protested her tears began to fall.

Colin's voice turned hard. "He has hurt you again, hasn't he?"

Abigail shook her head to clear the memory away, refusing to think on it more. Instead of dredging up the past, she needed to focus on the present and on what she must do now.

Leaving the ballroom, she felt the need for fresh air. She went down the last flight of stairs and hoped to find a backdoor that would lead to the gardens. As she made her way along the corridor, she glanced into a lovely sitting room. Perhaps she would find Lady Bedford inside and could simply ask how to get out to the gardens.

The drawing room was quite large, yet unoccupied. An empty fireplace graced one end, lording over several chairs and settees. The far wall boasted three giant windows stretching nearly to the ceiling, each with curtains flanking the sides and two with padded benches beneath.

Upon closer inspection, Abigail noticed that the middle window was not truly a window at all, but French doors that opened to the outside. Exactly what she had wished to find.

"Oh, Abigail," Lady Bedford said as she entered the room. "Have you finished resting so soon?"

A quick breath, and Abigail assumed her character once more. She turned away from the near exit with a gracious smile for her hostess. "I can never truly rest when in a new place. There is too much to explore and discover."

Lady Bedford smiled. "I am so pleased that you feel comfortable enough to do so. Come sit and join me."

"Thank you."

"It is so quiet these days, something I find I'm ill-suited for. My mama and sisters are away on holiday. They ought to be back in time for the dinner party we are hosting next week. And Diana, Timothy's sister, recently married. It was wholly unexpected, I assure you, though welcome. Yet, it has all left me quite to myself."

Abigail wondered at the lady's words. She cherished being alone, as it meant freedom, however momentarily, from her father's suffocating demands. Yet this woman seemed quite lost to be left to herself.

"I shall certainly try to ease some of your boredom, my lady."

The butler entered with a note on a tray, which Lady Bedford then read. "Oh dear," she sighed. "I am truly sorry, but it seems I am needed elsewhere. I volunteer with our local doctor when he finds himself overwhelmed with patients."

True shock marred Abigail's features. "Lord Bedford allows that?" She couldn't help but ask.

Lady Bedford's eyes widened. "Allows?" She laughed stiltedly, and Abigail knew she had hit upon a sensitive subject. "In point of fact, it was my only stipulation for marrying him. Thankfully, Timothy loves me enough not to prevent me from helping in whatever way I can." Taking Abigail's hand, she earnestly sought her eyes. "My dear, when the time comes for you to marry, let it be to a man who will not stifle you in any way."

Only after she was gone did Abigail realize her misstep in allowing her persona to slip. Lady Bedford had drawn out a bit of Abigail's true character. Hopefully not enough to have been noticed. She would need to focus harder so as to not allow that kind-hearted woman to strip her of her defenses.

Pleasant and demure, not distrustful and naive.

A commotion in the entryway drew her attention. Peeking out the door of the drawing room, Abigail was surprised to find two gentlemen greeting Lady Bedford on her way out. She greeted one with a quick kiss, surprising Abigail once more. Of course the gentleman must be her husband, the Marquess of Bedford, yet such forward behavior in the company of others was not often well received, at least to Abigail's understanding. Though to be fair, she had spent precious little time with members of the gentry.

The second gentleman looked on, not with contempt at their antics, but with an almost sad-looking smile, if such a thing was possible. Abigail had a moment of recognition. No, she did not remember having seen this man before. She thought it must rather be the pull of attraction, for he was remarkably handsome with light hair and a smile that could weaken the knees. It was not long, however, before he too was greeted with a warm kiss on the cheek.

"I do hope you don't mind, my dear," Lord Bedford was saying, his voice easily carrying down the length of the entryway. "I found Colin in desperate need of a holiday and dragged him home with me."

Colin? It could not be *her* Colin. She must be imagining a connection as she had been so recently thinking of her friend from so long ago.

Knowing she ought not to be eavesdropping, she inched the door forward, closing it all but the tiniest crack, just wide enough for her to peer through.

"Mind?" Lady Bedford dismissed the notion. "I couldn't be more thrilled. With Mother and my sisters away at present the house has been dreary as a tomb." She turned fully toward Colin. "In point of fact, I have a dear friend visiting as well, whom I would so love to introduce to you."

Abigail could not see the lady's face, but could hear the warmth in her words.

'Dear friend?' This will be easier than I thought. Her task would be nigh impossible without having the trust of those involved. With effort, Abigail drew her attention back to the conversation at hand. One never knew what information would prove useful over time. And knowledge was more powerful than anything.

"...and would it not be simply wonderful for you to form an attachment at last? You shall have no problem causing her to fall in love with you."

Fall in love with him? Not likely. She needed to keep her mind on her purpose. She could ill afford to allow a man to interfere in any way. Besides, her heart was safe, as it had been given away years ago. However, this conversation had indeed turned out to be useful, as it laid bare what could be expected of her. She would play the part of the lover, receiving any and all of this man's attentions, and no one would suspect her of anything.

The gentleman smiled indulgently. "My charms must be impressive indeed for you to have such faith in my abilities. But I assure you, I have no intention of causing anyone to fall in love with me."

Lord Bedford laughed. "You ought to be flattered my wife thinks so highly of that Haverford charm."

Abigail's knees wavered, nearly giving way beneath her. Grasping for a handhold she inadvertently closed the door, the noise reverberating down the long corridor, no doubt heard by those in the entry.

Colin Haverford. It was *her* Colin. Here. But how? Abigail had resigned herself to the fact that she would never see him again. She had made her peace with it long ago, had she not? And yet, the ghost of him in her past haunted her even now.

Unable to remain, on the off chance that he would enter this room, she stood and ran to the French doors leading outside. She fled to the garden, and into the copse of trees beyond. She needed time to think before being confronted with him.

Chapter 2

Colin Haverford, the Viscount Haverford, glanced down the corridor, thinking he had heard a door closing. Probably a servant. Turning back to his friends, the Marquess of Bedford and his wife, he saw that Eliza's gaze had not wavered.

"I have had your charm directed at myself in the past," she stated with a knowing smile. "I remember how flattering it can be."

Colin felt his face flush, a sensation uncommon since reaching manhood. Ever had he been comfortable with who he was, rarely wishing to be anything more. Had Eliza been this forthright in London? Surely not. Perhaps becoming mistress of Edgemont had boosted her confidence. Although, strictly speaking, their interactions had been few, especially when considering how comfortable they were in one another's company.

Timothy laughed upon seeing Colin's expression, which must have been one of confusion. "Come now,

Eliza. Let us allow Colin to at least brush the dust from his boots before marrying him off, shall we?"

It was Eliza's turn to redden. "Of course. You must excuse me, Colin. It has been a bit lonesome since Mama took the girls to London, and with our mourning I seem to have forgotten how to be amongst polite society. It has only been a week since we put off full mourning."

"There is nothing to forgive," Colin assured. "Now that I am in residence, we shall liven up this place and you shall have all manner of diversions."

"That shall have to wait, unfortunately." She turned back to Timothy. "I have been summoned by Doctor Peterson. I do apologize that I cannot stay now that you have arrived."

"I understand," Timothy said with an indulgent smile. "Go on, but send word to let me know when I may expect you."

Colin turned away as they whispered their farewells, allowing them a modicum of privacy. It was not long before Eliza was gone, and Colin followed Timothy up the stairs.

"I feel I must warn you," Timothy said with a sideways glance. "Eliza is planning a small gathering with the local gentry in a few days. She wishes to introduce you to the local young ladies."

Colin groaned. "Have you not explained my situation to her?"

Timothy sighed. "I have, and I warned her that you would not be so easily set off task."

"You certainly were not when you were in the throes of love," Colin replied, turning from his friend to gaze out the window of the guest chamber they had entered.

"Love?" Timothy's brows rose in genuine surprise. "I was under the impression that you simply wished to help the poor soul. Have I so thoroughly misjudged your interest? Colin, it has been ten years since you last laid eyes on the girl. And even then, you only met her a few dozen times." He shook his head. "I confess to not comprehending your fascination for this woman."

"I cannot claim to understand it myself," he said. Putting a finger at his throat, he loosened his cravat slightly. "You must believe that if I were to choose, I would gladly take a bride and join you as a sappy husband." Under his breath he added, "Unfortunately, I gave my heart away long ago and it has yet to return to me."

"Marriage has been ridiculously kind to me, I must admit. I sincerely wish you to have the same happiness, my friend."

Colin smiled, yet it carried with it a note of sadness. "Back to the issue at hand. Are you certain that Eliza will not let slip what I am after? For instance, to this 'dear friend' who is visiting?"

Timothy chuckled. "To be truthful, I do not know when Eliza became so attached to Miss Newell. They were introduced in London, shortly before our betrothal, and now she is a guest in my home. I have yet to meet her myself as I have been away in London with you. I do, however, trust Eliza implicitly. She would never betray your confidence." Timothy paused. "Have you considered what you will do when you see Miss Wallace again?"

Colin moved to a basin and poured water into it from a nearby pitcher. Only after he had splashed his face with some of the tepid liquid did he answer. "I confess, I have not allowed myself to think on it. I know what I will *wish* to do, but I do not often believe in accosting unsuspecting females with my unadulterated adoration."

Timothy laughed, easing the tension within the chamber. "Of course, no one would want that." He clasped his hands together. "In all seriousness, though, you must consider the possibility that she has changed since you knew her last. You must not lose your head before you have the chance to avenge the wrongs done to your family. As much as I wish it otherwise, she may not be trustworthy."

After a pause in which Colin refused to engage, Timothy straightened. "I shall leave you to it. I am anxious to see my son. I hear they change dramatically within the first few months and I wish to see if that is true. Then, I ought to check in with my steward to see how the estate has fared in my absence. I shall see you at dinner?"

"Absolutely. I shall be dressed to perfection, and anxiously awaiting my introduction, assuming our valets arrive in time." Colin and Timothy had ridden ahead of the carriage that was conveying their valets as well as their trunks, leaving them with no true way of knowing when the latter would arrive.

Moving to the window, Colin thought on what to do in the meantime. His room overlooked the gardens which were rather formal for his taste, but he knew Eliza would likely take them in hand over the next few years and, he hoped, make them more welcoming. He enjoyed a stroll through a good garden, and Edgemont knew him as a frequent visitor.

As he watched, he saw a woman pacing within the walled-off garden. Her head was bent, denying him more than a slight idea of her appearance, yet he could see by her dress that she was no servant. It must be Eliza's friend. What was her name? Had he forgotten it so quickly? Or had he not been informed of it as yet?

Her hands were in constant motion as she walked, as if she was deep in conversation, yet he saw no one nearby. How peculiar.

Making new acquaintances had always thrilled Colin. He found people fascinating in their differences. What sort of a person would this woman prove to be? And would she hinder his current plans? He would need to make that assessment soon, before anything could hinder his investigation. Nothing would stop him from locating Mr. Wallace.

Turning away, he made his way to the library, intent on finding suitable reading material. If his plan was to succeed, he would need to familiarize himself with the lay of the surrounding area as well as brushing up on the local gentry. Thankfully he was already quite familiar with Timothy's land; it was the surrounding country he was unsure of. Cursing Eliza's benevolence, he knew she would be of great assistance had she not run off to assist the local doctor. Who could say in what way she could actually provide assistance in such an area as medicine, but Timothy seemed to love her more for her efforts.

Pulling the now-tattered parchment from his trouser pocket, he read it to himself once more.

My Lord,

I am pleased to inform you that we have tracked Christopher Wallace to Shropshire. He is currently being surveilled by two of my finest runners who will continue in such endeavors until such time as they receive further instructions. I have taken the liberty, knowing that you would wish to travel to that location upon hearing this news, of arranging a meeting at the coaching inn of Freemont Glenn on Wednesday next during the dinner hour. My men will make themselves known to you upon your arrival.

______*D. Kenton*

He had received the missive three days prior and had not rested as he made hasty preparations to quit London and make his way to Shropshire. It was fortuitous indeed that Wallace had retreated to the county presided over by Colin's close friend and confidant. And Timothy had been away from his new bride for longer than he wished and was happy to travel with Colin in order to reunite with his wife.

It still rankled after all these years to yet be searching for Wallace. How could one man be so elusive? Although, to be fair, it was not the man himself that was so very difficult to find. No, Colin had known of Christopher Wallace's location many times through the years. It was the man's daughter who could never be located. Wallace must have secreted Abigail away somewhere, yet Colin was no closer to discovering where she was now than he had been at the start. At one time the woman was in London, however that had been a short-lived advantage as she had slipped away before Colin could seek her out.

Entering the library he pushed his frustration aside. Timothy had a fine collection, much larger than the one Colin claimed in either London or his own estate in Somerset. Certainly he would be able to find what he needed here. As he perused the book titles on the shelves, he struggled to focus on what he was seeing as he was assaulted by unbidden memories.

"Take it," he demanded.

"You know I cannot." Abigail attempted to push the book back into his hands.

Colin looked away, shame filling him. "You can't read?"

She punched his chest, hard. It was an act unbecoming of a girl, yet it made him like her all the more.

"Of course I can read. I am no simpleton."

He was grateful for the darkness as he felt his face flush, something all too common in Abigail's presence. "Then what is it? Surely not the cost. As the viscount's son you know I can afford it."

Abigail took a few steps away, silent. Understanding stirred, and Colin followed her, placing a hand on her shoulder. "He wouldn't like it, would he?"

Turning around, Abigail buried her head in Colin's chest, and the feelings that arose there had nothing to do with the pain of her attack a moment before. His arms wrapped around her and he dropped the book on the sand in order to hold her closer. She tensed, but did not move away. Colin loosened his grip, recognizing the sign of her pain.

"Why do you remain with him?" Colin whispered. "Come with me and I will hide you."

Abigail breathed deeply as she withdrew. "Hide me where? Besides your family, you have servants roaming everywhere. I would be caught."

"Then marry me," he said earnestly. "No one would question your right to be there if we were wed."

Abigail laughed and Colin recoiled at the sound. "Colin," she said softly, placing a hand on his cheek, lessening the pain of rejection. "You are eighteen. Do not be ridiculous."

"It is not ridiculous to want to save you."

Her hand moved to the back of his neck and she pulled him down to meet her. Her lips met his, cold and hesitant. She tasted of salt from the sea spray and something else he could not identify. Having never before kissed a girl, he was unsure how to respond, yet wanting more, he pulled her closer.

"Ahh!" she cried out, instant tears running down her cheeks.

He must have held her too tightly. Angry at his carelessness, he realized he ought to have known better. Her father never could keep his hands off his daughter, leaving welts and bruises in their wake.

Collecting herself a little, she shook her head. "You cannot save me from him." She turned and ran into the night.

Bending over, he picked up the book and brushed it free of sand. The thought of her constant pain lit a fire in his soul. He knew going after her now would be fruitless, as she would easily arrive home before he could catch her.

It was late and would not do for him to alert her father to her absence.

In the morning he would speak with his father and together they would come up with a solution. Letting the book slap his leg with each step, he made for home.

He would *save her. For one thing was certain, this first kiss would not be the last that they shared.*

That night, ten years prior, had been the last he had seen of Abigail. When he awoke the next day it was to his disgruntled father, storming about how his steward had run off taking the lion's share of funds from the estate. They were hardly left destitute, yet the theft had been considerable. It had taken his father years to recoup the loss.

Colin had been devastated. Not due to the missing fortune, but the steward had been Abigail's father, and the man would never have left without her. His love was gone, and Colin had no power to go after her.

Shaking off the memories, Colin finally found what he sought, *The Peerage of the United Kingdom of Great Britain and Ireland* by John Debrett, seventh edition. Precisely what he needed to familiarize himself with the local gentry. Taking it to a chair near the corner of the room he focused his study for the entire afternoon, only putting it down when it was time to prepare for dinner. Such a single-minded effort was further proof as to the extent of his feelings for Abigail, as he had not studied this hard since sitting for his exams at Eton. Entering his chamber he saw that his valet had indeed arrived and was busy unpacking Colin's trunks.

"Have you something suitable for me to wear this evening, Morley?" he asked, not certain there had been time for the man to press the wrinkles of travel out of anything.

His valet scoffed. "I would not be much of a valet if not, now would I, my lord?"

Morley made short work of getting Colin dressed. Exiting his room, he approached the staircase, intending to descend to the drawing room before being called into dinner. Glancing behind him, he flipped a tail of his coat which had folded up at the end. Upon turning forward once more he halted. Standing before him at the top of the stairs, unbelievable as it seemed to him, was Abigail.

His Abigail. His heart constricted and for a moment he forgot how to breathe. Studying her, he drank in every detail. Her reddish-brown hair was pulled back, her face framed with curls. Looking upon her face, Colin wondered how he had survived ten long years without seeing her. His attraction to her had somehow grown through the years and it took all of his inward strength to resist pulling her into his arms now. Abigail stared back at him with eyes somewhat guarded, causing him a moment of unease before he recalled himself and bowed.

"Good evening," he said. Unable to think of what else to say, he simply awaited her response.

Blinking rapidly, she broke her own stare and dipped into a curtsy. "Pardon me, my lord, but we have not been properly introduced."

'Properly introduced?' What the devil was the woman playing at? Was she not as baffled by their meeting as he? Or could she truly not remember him? He had certainly changed some in the intervening years. His shoulders were broader and he was no longer a gangly youth. She had changed as well, though not beyond recognition. Her hair was slightly darker and her skin a bit lighter as if she spent less time in the sun, and her eyes seemed to be shutting him out somehow.

Attempting a light-hearted air, he laughed to hide his confusion. "Perhaps you would allow me to escort you down so that our mutual friends might provide such an introduction."

"Thank you," she nodded, placing her hand lightly upon his arm.

Squinting at her from the corner of his eye, he led her down the grand staircase. "I must say there is something familiar about you. Have we not met before?" he asked pointedly.

She averted her eyes. "I do not believe so. You must be mistaken, or perhaps you have me confused with someone else."

"Hm." It was gratifying to know that he could still recognize when she was lying. What cause could she have to conceal the truth from him? "Where are you from? Perhaps I have ventured there."

Her grip on his arm tightened briefly as if he caught her by surprise, but it was a fairly benign question.

"I am lately come from London, my lord."

"London!" he repeated. Perhaps now he could get some information from her. "Why, our paths may have crossed any number of times. Might I have seen you at Almack's?"

She huffed. "Across a crowded ballroom? I hardly think you would remember if that were the case."

"You may not realize how memorable you truly are," he said quietly.

She paused midstep, and turned, eying him thoughtfully. Was she fighting a smile? What secret delight was she experiencing? She blinked, and her expression went devoid of all emotion. How was that possible? It must have been a skill she had developed since he had known her.

"Memory is an interesting thing," she said as they continued toward the drawing room. "For it is the meaning behind it that determines how lasting or vivid the memory remains."

"There you are," Eliza said as they entered the drawing room, though it was unclear which one of them she was addressing.

"Yes," Collin replied. "I found this lovely creature roaming about upstairs and thought I ought to guide her back to you."

Eliza's brow scrunched, curiosity written plainly across her face, yet it was Abigail who spoke.

"It appears to be quite easy to get turned around in such a large place," she said, releasing his arm as she curtsied to their hosts.

Colin smiled and bowed through his introduction to Miss Newell, a name he did not recognize. Just what was Abigail about? Why was she here, in Timothy's home, masquerading as someone else? His curiosity truly piqued, he studied her interaction with his friends. He decided that she was not the only one who could play games.

Chapter 3

A fitful night's rest was all Abigail could hope for at the best of times. It came as no surprise to her now that she was uneasy sleeping in a strange new bed in this house that fell just shy of being a palace. Her usual nightmares were replaced tonight as her mind was racing with questions.

The most pressing of all involved Colin. She had been certain he would recognize her, yet when he had failed to, she had panicked. Why had she not told him who she was? Panicking, she could think of nothing but to feign ignorance. It was indeed the easier path in that moment. Squeezing her eyes shut she berated herself once more for her idiocy. She was stuck, for how could she repent of her actions now? She would look the fool. Knowing that Colin, after all of these years, would see her that way was more than she could bear.

"Has he truly forgotten me?" she asked herself. The possibility burned a hole deep in her soul. Their acquaintance had been such that never had such a possibility crossed her mind.

Or, more than likely, she had changed over the past decade. She needed no looking glass to know of the shadows that surrounded her eyes from years of disturbed sleep, or to feel the gauntness in her face caused by a lack of appetite. Perhaps if she made a concerted effort to eat more, she would look similar to what she had before. The sleep, well, that was out of her control. Yet, for all her flaws, a quick perusal of her face showed mature features where once had been the lushful glow of youth.

Although, in the dim light of a lone candle she did look the spectre. The type that haunted children's dreams. It was no wonder Lady Eliza had taken pity on her, inviting her to the country. If only a holiday could take away the nightmare that was her life. Tossing on the bed, she chuckled at her own foolishness, yet she could not shake her concerns.

Now that Colin thought her a stranger, would she be able to maintain the pretense? She had trembled all through dinner, convinced that Colin would at any moment realize who she was. At one point, she spilled her wine on the table causing a ruckus as the footmen rushed into action cleaning it up. Although embarrassed, it had granted her the perfect opportunity to excuse herself for the evening. She had needed time to put her thoughts in order.

Through the years she had imagined their reunion countless times. She had always dreamed of rushing into his outstretched arms, allowing him to enshroud her in safety and love. He would renew his offer of marriage, of course, now that they were old enough for such a thing. They would kiss once more, reliving her most cherished memory. And he would keep her safe from her father, never allowing him to hurt her again.

Yet, the actuality of their reunion had borne no resemblance to her dreams. And now she did not know how to proceed. She must act the part of falling for his charms; easy enough as it would likely be real. Yet, could she do it while simultaneously keeping her identity a secret? She had often silently prided herself in her acting ability, the same mastery that often allowed her to disappear in the midst of a crowd. A prowess that had been untested to this magnitude. It would take all of her skill indeed to mislead Colin, as she knew him to be clever.

Well before the sun's first rays began to trace across the blackened sky, she gave up all hope of sleep. Reality was a harsh master, yet she could not ignore it. What would Colin do if he were to find out her true purpose in being at Edgemont? Cast her out? Likely. Send her to prison? He ought to. Deport her to some godless country filled with criminals? Heaven forfend! The Colin who had wished to save her was in the past. He could have changed in any number of ways over the years, and his affection for her had likely lessened. And if that were not the case it hardly mattered. Her father had found her when she had left no clues as to her whereabouts. If she were to be with Colin, it would simply make her that much easier to find.

No, she could not count on Colin saving her. She would need to rely on herself alone, and the only way she could appease her father was with the Marchioness's jewels.

She needed something to do, some occupation to help her escape such dreary thoughts. Slipping into her dressing gown, she brushed her hair behind her back and crept to the door. Members of the *ton* were notoriously late sleepers, and the servants would not be up for another hour at least, making this the perfect time to snoop.

Lady Eliza's jewels were likely kept in her dressing room. That would be difficult to obtain access to, especially if the lady had slept in her own bed. There was, of course, the possibility that she would have spent the night with her husband in his chambers. The thought brought heat to Abigail's cheeks, her being alone notwithstanding. The marquess and his wife seemed by all outward appearances to be quite fully in love with one another, however, Abigail was loath to take such a chance this morning. Being discovered in her scheme was out of the question.

There was no need to take foolish chances as her father could scarcely expect her to return victorious after less than an entire day. Surely she could take some time to accomplish her task with care.

No, today she would continue her perusal of the estate. Perhaps she would stumble on something else of value that would placate her father. Heaven knew she needed to keep him happy. He had made it abundantly clear what the consequences would be were she to fall out of favor with him. She shivered, an action having nothing to do with the chill in the air. Although, to fall out of favor, one would think it necessary to be in favor first, which was something Abigail had never thought of herself.

Slipping through her door, she glanced down the corridor. Unfortunately, or perhaps it was for the best, it was too dark to see if anyone lurked beyond the few feet surrounding her. Perfect. As long as she could see no one, it stood to reason that no one would see her. Her bare feet made nary a sound as she crept slowly along the corridor, not wishing to crash into any furniture lurking in the shadows.

Without a candle to light her way, she trailed her hand along the wall to her left, using it to guide her past rooms she now knew truly to be unoccupied. Even so, she slowed her steps even more and held her breath as she passed their doorways.

"Why is darkness always accompanied by a feeling of being watched?" she muttered softly.

Even in the absence of his presence, Abigail imagined her father's rank breath on the nape of her neck, as if he himself were guiding her footsteps toward the treasure he so desperately desired.

It would never be enough. She knew that even now. She could hand over all the diamonds and emeralds of the *ton,* including the queen's jewels, and he would still yearn for more. He would still assert his rightful claim to them. The people who stood in the way of his pursuits meant nothing to him, including Abigail herself. Although he claimed his hope that she would finally prove herself useful with this, her first real opportunity.

Inching down one flight of stairs brought her near the marquess's study. Likely locked, but worth a try. Without a sound she grasped the handle, surprise filling her as the door easily swung open. Her shock held her immobile for a moment, then she slid just as silently within and shut the door once more.

Pausing, she leaned back against the door. Her breaths came quick and shallow and she focused on calming them. Once she did so, she remained for a moment more, listening for any sounds of a stirring household. Hearing nothing but the roar of her own heart, she stepped to the desk.

Without a light she was unlikely to recognize anything which could prove helpful, yet she squinted over the loose pages that lay scattered across the desktop. Attempting to read anything in the darkness proved fruitless as she could make nothing out.

"A search with no clear purpose is little more than wishful thinking," she whispered, straightening up. Yet she could not give up. The unlocked door might very well be an oversight that the butler or some other servant would remedy in the future and she would likely never have such an opportunity again.

There was nothing for it. She needed a light. Opening the top drawer she was relieved to feel the necessary supplies. Lighting the lone candle that rested on the corner of the desk, her eyes painfully protested before adjusting to the admittedly dim glow.

She quickly rummaged through the pages that she now recognized as accounting sheets like many she had seen scattered across her father's varying desks over the years. The numbers she glimpsed were staggering, yet did not seem terribly outlandish given the breadth of the marquess's supposed holdings. How did the aristocracy possibly manage such vast assets?

Opening another drawer revealed a pile of papers scraps, each with writing scrawled upon it. Picking up a few, Abigail fought back a laugh.

Her eyes of brown have in my mind grown…

The figure arose as she accepted my rose…

Time will not tarnish that which we choose to varnish…

Line after line of drivel. Yet, the idea that a man as prestigious and powerful as the marquess attempting poetry as a way to express his love and devotion for another was endearing, and Abigail felt a sudden kinship with the man, as it reminded her of another long-ago night.

"I simply do not know what good it will do me," Colin said. He was home from school until after the new year, yet he could not seem to leave school behind.

"Perhaps none," Abigail said with a laugh. "For who would wish to court you? At fifteen you are little more than a child."

Colin huffed and straightened his shoulders. "I'll have you know that as a future viscount I am already quite sought after."

"Only by Sissy Carlisle, and she seeks anyone with a title."

Colin scrambled as he stood in a rush, obviously intent on leaving. Not wishing to see him go so soon, Abigail also stood as she attempted to placate him.

"I am sorry," she rushed to say. "I ought not to tease you so, but Colin, you are so serious! You need to laugh more, have more fun."

Taking a few steps, Colin then turned back. "I need to learn this, Abigail."

"Whatever for?" she asked in her most aristocratic voice, still attempting to draw out his smile. "Poetry cannot help you run an estate."

"No, but…" he hesitated.

"But, what?" she asked, taking his hand in her own, truly wishing to understand.

He stared at their clasped hands for a moment before answering. "Suppose I do wish to court a lady someday. What will she think if I cannot even write a simple poem?"

No longer feeling the urge to laugh, Abigail squeezed his hand. "Sit back down, Colin. I will help you." Even as she agreed to help, a strange new emotion filled her. The thought of Colin caring for another stabbed through her making her regret the offer. Pushing aside her confusing emotions, she helped him as best she could.

They had laughed over silly rhymes about anything they could think of for over an hour, and Abigail to this day could not pick up a volume of poetry without thinking of that night. It was the first time she had recognized her feelings for what they truly were, something she had been unable to forget.

Placing the papers back into the drawer, she closed it almost reverently. Feeling a deeper respect for the marquess than she thought possible upon such short acquaintance, once more drew out remorse for what she must do.

Opening the next drawer her breath caught. Within sat a slender, ornately carved wooden box, the type Abigail had seen displayed in some of the higher end jewelry shop windows in London. Not that she would ever have had occasion to venture within such establishments, yet she did enjoy looking.

With an unsteady hand she reached in to extract the treasure. A small clasp, easily undone, allowed her to lift the lid, only to find disappointment. There were no jewels within, no ornately set gems on a necklace chain, no matching earbobs. Just a slightly crumpled, folded bit of parchment. Nothing of value which she could turn over to her father and hopefully move on to someplace new, away from Colin and his friends. For as much as it may hurt her to leave him again, it was the only way she could assure his safety from her father's wrath.

Curiosity warred with disappointment as she withdrew the paper, carefully unfolding it and laying it flat on the desk. Moving the candle closer to avoid straining her eyes, she read:

My dearest Timothy,

The day of our wedding fast approaches and I find myself torn between the necessary preparations with little time to complete them and my desire to simply be with you, which cannot come soon enough. Mama is beside herself with joy while Clara has informed me of her imminent visit to your purportedly large library. Of course, she wishes us both happiness, yet her desire to constantly be reading begins to worry me. Perhaps once we are wed you may help in turning her head toward other pursuits.

Why would the marquess keep such a letter of seemingly little significance?

Papa continues to decline. He no longer leaves his room, and rarely arises from his bed. Doctor Rogers assures us that the end is near, yet can anyone truly be ready to say their final goodbyes to those they truly love? My only consolation is that he will soon bid adieu to his pain...

What must it have been like for this woman to have been raised by a loving father? Abigail could only guess as she read on.

My soul longs now to be reunited with you, to bask in your comforting arms. The home we shall create together shall carry all the love and devotion that others aspire to. I dream of children, your children who shall be raised as I was, with loving parents who are devoted to one another...

Guilt of reading such private sentiments washed over her, yet she continued on, determined to discover why such a letter would be housed in so ornate a container. Once finished it seemed the contents of the missive must have held significant meaning to the owner for their sentimentality alone, hence the protection of the box. Seeds of longing for such a love had long since been planted within her own breast, keeping alive the hope that Colin represented.

It became obvious to her then, that there was nothing for her here. Perhaps if she were a more accomplished thief, she would have found something. Sitting in the desk chair as if she belonged there, she wondered what she was doing. Lady Eliza had shown true kindness in inviting Abigail to stay. Even in the midst of her grief from losing her father the lady had thought not of herself, but of Abigail's needs. Could such selflessness truly exist? And was Abigail to repay such kindness through theft and deceit? How could she betray Lady Eliza in such a way?

"How can I do otherwise?" she whispered aloud.

Abigail had no family other than her father, no relations or friends who could take her in. She had no skills with which to earn a living, and precious little money to live on. Her father was her sole means of survival. There simply was no other choice. Her conscience had no place here. It would be best to ignore its protests. Yet the more she knew of the marquess and his wife, the harder her task appeared.

A sound from the corridor drew her eyes to the closed door. Extinguishing the candle, she slipped off the chair and crouched under the desk, afraid to even breathe. Heart pounding, she struggled to hear over it. Convinced she would be caught, she wondered what she could possibly say in her defense. Her mind remained a blank slate as she awaited the snick of the door opening.

It never came.

After what felt like an age, Abigail struggled out from underneath the desk and stood. The darkness outside the window seemed to have lightened a touch since she had first arrived in the room. It was time to leave, else she would be caught by the servants beginning their morning tasks.

Gratefully, she met no one else as she returned to her room. For the next little while, her only concern was whether to continue being a coward and ask for a tray in order to avoid Colin for a while longer, or to descend for breakfast.

Chapter 4

"Abigail is here!" Colin declared upon entering Timothy's study, arms stretched wide in victory. It had taken every ounce of his self-control to keep this information to himself since his discovery the previous evening. The relief he felt in the sharing was evident as he flopped into a wingback chair facing his friend.

Timothy's head rose above his ledger. "I am aware," he said slowly. "Is that not what brought you to Shropshire?"

"I do not mean here in Shropshire," he leaned forward, relishing this moment of revelation, "but rather here in Edgemont."

"You cannot be in earnest," Timothy protested, granting Colin his undivided attention. "I would know if she were within my household, surely."

"Nevertheless, it is true." His satisfied smirk was in full form this morning.

"No," Timothy stated in disbelief, a furrow on his brow. "I am quite certain we have not employed an Abigail Wallace."

"She is not a servant," Colin said, savoring this information. "She is a guest."

Timothy's eyes nearly popped from his head. "You are speaking of Miss Newell?"

"Indeed I am."

Timothy rose and paced to the window. "I am at an utter loss," he muttered, then turned back to face Colin. "Why did you say nothing last evening?"

Colin leaned forward in his chair. "You must believe it was one of the more difficult things I have accomplished within my lifetime. However, she feigned ignorance when we met in the corridor. I do not know the reason, yet I decided to play along."

"What reason could she have to lie? Eliza and I have no acquaintance with her father, and I do not believe that his reputation is as widespread as to warrant a separation from his name. Would she have come here knowing that you would come?"

"I do not see how she would know. I did not plan on coming here until the day before we left London. And if she came for my benefit, why deny who she is? Besides, she would have used a false name with Eliza since their introduction in order for her to maintain that name here."

"I do not like this," Timothy muttered, sitting back down at his desk. "That suggests a scheme. Deception in any form is not something I can allow. We must confront her."

Colin tensed. "If we confront her, what is to keep her from fleeing? Timothy, I have lost her once. Do not ask me to do it again."

Timothy's expression softened and Colin forced himself to relax once more.

"We are two relatively intelligent individuals," he said, attempting to lighten the mood. "If we work at it, I am confident we can discover what is going on here." Colin stood and took up Timothy's prior position at the window. "We know Christopher Wallace is a thief and a liar, although my experience with his daughter never led me to believe her capable of the same."

"Yes, well that was some time ago. People change. I confess I am not easy with the idea of her carrying on in this manner under my roof, having no knowledge of her possible schemes. For all we know she has been with Wallace since they left your estate and he has turned her head toward his own aims. I do not trust her."

"No, you have no reason to. As difficult as it is for me to admit, I find my trust in her shaken as well. Yet, know not what purpose her lying serves," he added hopefully. "It may not be as nefarious as you fear."

"Colin, we must tell Eliza. If her guest truly is Abigail, we must place her on her guard."

"Of course. Now that I have found Abigail there is no longer any reason to withhold this from your wife. I shall leave that task to you."

A movement down on the lawn caught Colin's attention. A woman strolled purposefully along, a parasol blocking her identity. She was heading toward the tree line of the small forest located on Timothy's property. Having explored nearly every inch of Edgemont over the years, he knew she would find a wonderful hidden meadow if she stayed true to her current course. The meadow had been left untouched by the late Marchioness, Timothy's mother, except for a solitary stone bench that had been placed on the perimeter. Wildflowers abounded in the space, and in the spring the aroma was quite intoxicating.

A knock on the door drew the attention of both men.

"Enter," Timothy called.

Eliza poked her head in the room as Timothy rose from his seat. “I am off to visit with Lady Morgan. I wondered if either of you would wish to accompany me?”

Timothy smiled, indulgently. “As it is unlikely for me to accomplish anything here, I think I shall.” He turned to Colin. “You remember Peter Morgan from University, I trust? He was a few years our senior. Quite a pleasant sort of man, he is currently caring for his aging mother. What say you, old man?”

Colin gave them both a fond smile. “I do remember him, although for now, I intend to spend some time with *Miss Newell* and see if I can discover what she is about.” As Eliza was here, the woman he had seen walking had to have been Abigail.

“Very well,” Timothy replied, ignoring Eliza’s questioning gaze. “We shall return before luncheon. I expect to be apprised of anything you discover.” Colin had no doubt that Eliza would know everything before the couple arrived at their neighbor’s estate.

Before long, Colin’s own horse was saddled and he made his way toward the hidden meadow. Curiosity drove him to see if Abigail had indeed found it, as well as her thoughts on the place. Besides his interest in her motives, he simply wished to spend time with her, as he had longed to for years.

Thoughts of enjoying her company spurred him faster. She had excused herself before dinner finished the previous evening, leaving him dissatisfied and yearning for more. Before she left, he had found his gaze drawn to her more than a few times. There was something about her that he could not quite name; something that worried him. Was it simply her appearance? Upon close inspection she did indeed appear to be somewhat ill. She seemed to be mostly in need of a host of solid meals and steady sleep, although Colin admittedly had no medical knowledge.

Now that Abigail was once more within arm's reach, he longed to spend every moment possible in her company. Where had she been all these years? What was she doing here? Where was Christopher Wallace? The questions seemed unending as he drew near the hidden meadow, yet they would have to wait. For as long as Abigail wished to keep up this pretense, he could not ask them of her.

Not wishing to frighten her with his approach, he dismounted before he arrived and tied his horse to a tree. Setting off on foot, he stole along as quietly as he could, a bit dissatisfied with the noise he still made. At the edge of the meadow, he paused and watched with interest as Abigail knelt in the center of the clearing, busying herself with something on the ground. A gentle humming reached his ears. What was the woman doing?

"Have you lost something, Miss Newell?" he asked, stepping out of the trees at last.

The humming stopped as her head whipped up. The woman's fair complexion was momentarily relieved by a healthy flush of color in response to being caught so off guard.

Rising to her feet, she rubbed at the dirt on her fingers. "You will think me silly, Lord Haverford."

A smile crept over his face. "You do not know me well, Miss Newell, but I assure you, I adore silly." He offered her his handkerchief to help clean her hands.

For a long moment their eyes met. In that time, nothing else mattered. Abigail was here, with him. Regardless of the games they played, they were together once more. Her eyes, though still somehow shadowed, seemed to draw him closer. Their grey was interspersed with flecks of green and gold. Her brows tensed, and Colin had the distinct impression that she was waging a war within. His heart raced as his eyes dropped to her lips.

"You are staring, Lord Haverford," she whispered.

Unable to decipher if she was pleased with the attention he took a step back, laughing uneasily. Right.

He was still Lord Haverford, not Colin. And she was Miss Newell. It would serve him well to remember that. "Forgive me, Miss Newell, but are you certain that we have never met? You seem quite familiar."

Miss Newell hesitated, seeming to weigh her words. "Would it matter, my lord?" she asked, sounding almost disappointed before he even answered.

"Perhaps not," Colin conceded. "And if you do not wish to tell me, I will press you no further." *At least not as plainly,* he thought. If she would not admit her identity, Colin would need to find another way of drawing her out.

She glanced up at him. "You think I am hiding something?" she asked coyly. Colin smiled, sensing her more playful tone, and being grateful for it.

His eyes narrowed shrewdly to cover the sincerity of his words. "I think there are a great many things that you are hiding, Miss Newell. The question is, to what end?" Clasping his hands behind his back, he rocked on the heels of his Hessians. "Now, will you not, at the very least, tell me why you were digging in the earth? For I find myself in need of some silliness just now."

The hint of a smile showed on Abigail's face as she looked at her stained hands, remnants of dirt still clinging to her skin and under her nails, despite his now ruined handkerchief. Her eye twitched, a barely perceptible movement, yet Colin took note.

"I have buried a wish, my lord."

Colin could not hide his excitement that it was nothing as benign as planting a flower or some such unnecessary task. Knowing it was not the truth did not diminish his keenness to hear her tell a tale.

"A wish?" he asked, eager for her to elaborate.

Her smile grew, yet she remained silent, increasing his curiosity all the more.

"I do hope you made it a good one," he said, tamping down his need to know more. Had she lost her taste for storytelling so quickly?

"I assure you, it is the best wish I have," she said earnestly.

"Have you many?"

The familiarity of their conversation further testified to their previous closeness. Conversation had always come easily for them, and the years seemed to be fading away as they spoke.

"Not as many as some, I would think." Abigail stooped and picked a clump of wildflowers. Smelling them, she succeeded in hiding the lower half of her face, denying Colin the opportunity to read her expression.

"Do you think me so fanciful?" he asked.

She turned and made her way to the lone stone bench. "Fanciful?" she repeated. "Not a bit. But I have yet to meet a man who did not long for more than he currently possessed. I hope you will forgive my assumption that you would be the same."

Following her indication he sat beside her, unsure whether he ought to be offended. Perhaps Abigail had forgotten her ruse of not knowing him, for this sort of candid conversation was not common among strangers, yet was familiar for the two of them. Either way, Colin measured his response. "I suppose I will have my work cut out for me to prove to you that men are not all such greedy creatures."

Her face flushed once more as she seemed to realize the offense inherent in her previous statement.

"Now, Miss Newell," he said, cutting her off from any response, "It takes more direct language than that to offend me, I assure you. Although, I would not be above requiring some form of payment for my good humor."

Her eyes clouded with instant distrust causing Colin to regret his playfulness. Her spine stiffened, and she quickly rose, one hand clasping at her chest as if she was out of breath. Knowing the sort of man her father was, it should come as no surprise to Colin that such a statement would draw out a strong physical response, and yet it did.

Abigail gave a quick curtsy. "I really ought to be getting back so I can rest before dinner."

"Forgive me," he said, grabbing her arm to stop her retreat. "It was not my intent to cause you alarm."

She laughed, albeit shakily and without mirth, and pulled her arm gently out of his grasp. "No, no. I am simply tired, and it is still a bit of a walk back to the house."

"Please, allow me to make it up to you." He indicated the way he had come into the meadow. "My horse is not far off. Allow me to fetch him so you may ride back to Edgemont, saving your energy." He reached for her arm once more, but she backed farther away. "Please, it is the least I can do. You have my word as a gentleman that I will get you back safely."

He could see the indecision in her eyes as they darted around. Her very demeanor testified of fear, but fear of what? Colin had never known her to be afraid of him, and he did not relish that feeling now. Not wishing to frighten her further, he exerted all of his patience waiting for her to respond.

"I suppose there can be no harm in that. Truly I am quite fatigued. Given the number of trees here, I rather doubt my ability to return on my own. I am, in fact, unsure the direction of the house from here." Her eyelids drooped low and her earlier color faded from her face as she sat once more. Seeing these rapid changes in her demeanor only heightened Colin's concern.

"I will send for the doctor upon our arrival," he suggested. "Perhaps he will have some sort of sleeping aid."

"No!" she nearly shouted, startling Colin with her vehemence. Taking a deep breath she added more calmly, "No, thank you. That won't be necessary."

"Very well," he said, keeping his confusion over her behavior to himself. "Wait here, and I will fetch my horse."

"Yes, thank you."

As he walked his thoughts tumbled. What was this woman about? There was an obvious need for rest, as well as nourishment, but was there more she suffered from? Why would anyone turn down aid when it was so plainly needed? Was it the cost? Given the amount of money Christopher Wallace had absconded with from Colin's family estate, there should be no need for Abigail to worry over such a thing. The thought that the scoundrel would not support his only daughter was deplorable.

If Wallace was not supporting Abigail, then who could be? Her clothing was the only real clue available to him. Her dresses seemed to be well made, yet nothing extravagant. While not of the latest fashion, the styles were easily still acceptable. Someone must be pulling Abigail's strings. And was this same person the cause of Abigail's ruse? The familiar feeling of needing to protect her resurfaced. Perhaps he was not capable of continuing this ruse without distressing her, and Colin realized he did not wish to continue this game any longer.

Chapter 5

Abigail had never experienced the luxury of having a maid. When she was young her mother had taught her manageable ways of styling hair, and she was always certain to have fairly simple dresses in which she could secure the fastenings herself. Her current wardrobe was an exception, and Abigail realized quickly how desperately she needed assistance.

Molly, who was proving herself expertly capable, was currently running a comb through Abigail's hair, causing the latter to wonder how she would ever go back to doing such things herself. Closing her eyes she basked in a sense of release. Of all her many worries, her coiffure need not be added to the pile.

Upon returning to her room after her unfortunate encounter with Colin she wish for more time to rest, yet the others would be expecting her in the breakfast room presently. Heaven knew that sleep would only do her good, yet it would need to wait. Sitting still, allowing

Molly to softly style detangle her locks, her eyelids drooped, and her attention wandered.

"Your hair is so soft, miss," Molly stated as she brushed. "My sister's little one has soft hair like this, softest you ever felt. Like silk from the Orient, I imagine. Once my uncle brought us some silk. He's a tailor, you see. Told Mama to fashion a dress for one of us; I have four sisters, you know. There was not nearly enough silk for all of us, and Mama could not decide who would get such a dress, so in the end she cut the silk and gave a piece to each of us. Now I have a lovely ribbon I keep for special occasions."

The prattle continued as Abigail's thoughts strayed once more back to Colin. Why could she think of nothing else? Her performance this morning in the clearing had nearly ended in disaster. And if he had known what she had truly buried? The thought made her stomach churn. Still, he had proved every bit as easy to converse with now as he ever had been and she had found herself sinking into old patterns, forgetting to be on her guard.

A silence fell over the room, drawing Abigail's eyes to Molly's through the looking glass. From the look on the young girl's face it was apparent that Abigail had missed some cue to answer or respond in some way.

"Forgive me," Abigail fumbled as she straightened in her seat. How careless to be so thrown off by a maid. Such a slip would surely cause some to wonder at her station. "I was woolgathering."

"Oh, goodness!" Molly exclaimed, obviously chagrined to have Abigail lower herself enough to apologize to a simple maid. "'T'is no matter, miss. I ought not to have gone on so. It is only that puppies make me so glad to be alive. I merely thought they might cheer you some as well. I own it is not my place to suggest such a thing, only you seem a bit low since coming to Edgemont. Mind you, I have no way of knowing your disposition prior..."

The poor girl continued on, once more requiring precious little additional input from Abigail, yet something had indeed sparked her interest. When the maid paused for breath, Abigail took the opening.

"What was that you said about puppies?"

"You see Sprocket, the master's favorite hunting hound, is down in the stables now giving birth to a litter of pups. I simply thought you might like to see them once they come."

Abigail, hardly hearing anything more through the rest of Molly's ministrations, rose and made her way out to the stables. Her interest had piqued indeed to see the puppies. Dogs had forever held a fascination for Abigail—their loyalty and devotion to their owners being something she yearned for. And how excited to be able to see something so new, freshly born into the world. The idea of something pure and unpolluted, so untouched by the cruelties that could certainly be leveled against them, fascinated her and drew her forward.

The stables were warm and muggy when Abigail entered moments later, causing her skirts to cling to her legs and beads of sweat to run down her back. Apart from the entryway, stalls for the animals ran down both sides of the long building with a walkway in the center.

"Camden, find me a blanket, we must warm this one." Lady Eliza's gentle voice could be heard easily over the low nickers of the horses in their stalls. A young boy ran out of a stall partway down the aisle, nearly colliding with Abigail as he passed.

Peeking around the corner of the stall, Abigail was greeted by one of the most serene scenes she could have imagined. Lady Eliza sat, unconcerned by the likely damage to her dress, beside the mother who was crowded by several other, much larger, pups as they suckled their first meal. A man knelt over the mother dog, watching that all was as it should be. In one hand, Lady Eliza gently held what appeared to be a miniature greyhound statuette. Yet even as she watched, Lady Eliza stroked the bundle with a gentle finger, eliciting a shudder from what was now clearly one of the new puppies.

"Oh," Abigail breathed, feeling her heart might break at the beauty of it all, her sigh catching the attention of those within. At the intrusion, the mother raised her head and growled weakly.

"Best to not come any closer, miss," the man warned, not unkindly. "Sprockett'l not take kindly to a stranger near her young'uns."

Abigail's face flamed as she muttered a quiet apology. She had not considered the ramifications of her presence. Instinct and longing had moved her forward. As long as she could remember Abigail had longed for a dog, an animal of her own that would act as both faithful companion and protector.

Lady Eliza smiled, conveying that she need not be concerned. Rising up on her knees, the lady ever so gently placed the tiny bundle next to the mother, who sniffed at the pup then turned away, clearly more interested in the others, upon whom she bestowed loving licks and gentle nudges. Abigail's heart lurched at the rejection.

"I fear you may be right about this pup, Gerard." Lady Eliza stood and brushed straw and dirt off her skirts. "See if you can get him to drink something tonight. Perhaps you could have Benet sit up with him. If the mother continues to reject him, there may not be much else that we can do." Exiting the stall, Lady Eliza took Abigail companionably by the arm and walked with her out of the stable. "He is the runt of the litter," she said by way of explanation.

"Does that entail more than simply being smaller than the others?" Abigail asked, concerned over the mother's apparent rejection.

"The dam has already refused to acknowledge the poor thing. Animals seem to know when a little one will not survive long. They do little to assist in such a situation. It all seems to be part of the natural instinct for each species." Lady Eliza's countenance remained perfectly calm, as though she had experience sharing such clinical information. "Aside from humans, I mean. We, of course, love our young regardless of size."

Lady Eliza's view on the natural state of parents loving their offspring must have been a direct result of her being raised by loving parents, something Abigail could scarcely fathom. Her mother had loved her, she supposed, though Abigail's memories of her were dim.

"Gerard and Benet will continue to work with both the animals throughout the night," Lady Eliza continued, "but I fear the mother has made her choice."

"What do you mean? What will happen to the puppy if the mother continues to reject him?"

"We will attempt to feed him, but without his mother's milk his chances are slim."

Abigail took a deep breath, hoping to still her rush of emotions. Lady Eliza stopped halfway to the house and looked directly at Abigail.

"It truly is best not to think on it overmuch. There is little that can be done, and beyond that it is out of our control."

"Out of our control," Abigail repeated. "I wonder…"

"Yes?"

"Well, is it not an instinctual behavior for mothers, if not all parents," *certainly not my father,* "to protect and care for their young?" The moment the words were free Abigail felt the fool. If she had learned nothing else in her childhood, it was clear that her father felt neither love nor responsibility for Abigail's happiness and well-being. Such naive thinking should have been behind her.

"Of course!" Lady Eliza stated, eyes wide with feeling. "I do not have much experience with animals. I have some experience with new mothers through my work with the hospital in London as well as my work with the doctor here. Each experience has shown me the purest love that a parent has for their offspring. Yet, as with most anything, there are exceptions. Sprocket knows that as the runt of the litter, that puppy has very little chance of survival. I believe she chooses to abandon the pup in defense of her own feelings. Can you imagine bonding with a child, a baby, only to know that he or she would survive mere days, possibly only hours? The heartbreak inherent in such a situation must be immense. I believe Sprocket has chosen to close her heart in order to prevent the pain that will inevitably come."

Abigail stared unseeing for a moment, allowing Lady Eliza to guide her toward the house. Could such a rationalization be correct? And would that explanation carry for something other than a dog? Perhaps for her own father? Had something in her infancy convinced him he would be better off not loving his own daughter? Such a thought had never occurred to her until now. Perhaps her father had not always been so cold and distant. Granted, humans were not mere animals. Raised higher by superior intellect and the will of God, men were held to certain moral standards. Yet the love of a parent for their child still ought to be instinctual.

All of it was hypothetical, and would likely remain so, as her father would never willingly be so open and honest with her. And having no knowledge of her parents' lives before she came along meant she had no insight into what could have caused her father to be what he was.

Was it foolish to wish to see him in a more favorable light? It would certainly be a one-sided effort as he had made his feelings for her clear long ago.

"Abigail, are you unwell?" Lady Eliza's kind inquiry snapped Abigail back to the current conversation.

"Oh, no," she answered. "It is curious, is it not, how easily one's thoughts can run away with them? I apologize for being so easily distracted." She hoped her smile could ease the tension the current conversation had built up.

"Rubbish. Friends have no need to apologize. And we are, you know." Eliza laid a hand on Abigail's arm. "Friends, I mean. I hope you know that."

Friends?

Abigail's heart constricted within her chest, mimicking the squeeze on her arm, so much so that she barely contained the urge to grasp at it. Gazing at Eliza, she felt the truth of it. Uncertain how to respond to such an idea, she turned and looked back toward the stable. "If only there was more we could do."

"Pray, Abigail," Lady Eliza responded. "One can always pray."

Chapter 6

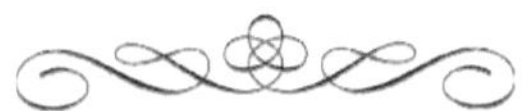

"Might I have a word, Eliza?" Colin asked meekly from the doorway to the drawing room.

"Certainly," she responded, turning to face him and taking a seat. "I do hope there is not a problem with your accommodations."

Finding no other occupants, and wishing not to be overheard, he closed the door behind him, drawing a raised eyebrow from the lady.

"No, no. Everything is splendid." He took a quick breath, hoping to not overstep his bounds as a guest. He considered Eliza a friend, though they had not spent much time together since her marriage to Timothy. He had kept himself busy with his search for Abigail, as well as fulfilling his duties in the House of Lords. Sitting down across from her now, he could not help but chuckle at her concerned expression. "It is nothing so serious as to cause such alarm, I assure you. I simply wished to speak to you of Miss Newell."

Eliza's anxious eyes altered into an expression oddly reminiscent of Colin's mother just before she used to reprimand him for an offense, causing him to laugh once more.

"I wished to speak with you as well." She afforded a quick glance at the door before leaning slightly closer to him. Softly she whispered, "Abigail?"

"I see Timothy has spoken to you on this subject," he said with relief.

"I confess I am still baffled by all the secrecy. Are you not pleased to see her?"

"Of course, I am!" he answered, louder than he intended. "However, my pleasure is of little importance just now. First, we must ascertain her motives for being here. That is where you come in."

Eliza scoffed. "I can offer little assistance, as I scarcely know her. And from what Timothy tells me, what little I do know is all fabricated."

"That is precisely why I need you," he insisted. "You are in an ideal position to question her. She is here at your sole discretion, upon your invitation. As the lady of this estate, you have every right to delve into her background. Where is she from? Who are her family?"

"You realize, I assume, that any responses she gives to my questions would be contrived? What could you possibly learn from hearing her lies?"

"Perhaps nothing, yet my hope is that not every word out of her mouth will be false. Perhaps, as she becomes more at ease in your presence, she may falter and share some information that could prove useful."

"Who could prove useful?" Timothy asked as he entered the room, leaving the door open once more, Abigail entering nearly on his heels. She wore a solid green evening gown, most unlike the usual fabrics favored by members of the *ton* in its lack of embellishment. With no baubles or frills, simply a relatively simple patch of embroidery around the borders, it would have stuck out for what it lacked were it to be worn to a dinner in London. Nothing lacked in the cut of the gown itself, and the color flattered its wearer, so much so that Colin momentarily neglected to stand upon her entrance. Thankfully, Eliza came to his rescue.

"Rascal, the new pup," Eliza stated, "could be useful as a house dog." The lie rolled off her tongue easier than Colin would have guessed. "He might make a pleasant companion for someone, if he were taught."

Abigail's smile was immediate. "I must confess, I refused to allow Molly to assist me in dressing for dinner until she checked on the pups for me. She dutifully brought me word that the little one had been successful in drinking some milk this evening."

"Well, that is wonderful." Eliza's smile was broad and genuine, as she seemed to be taking quite well to her segue. "I was hoping for such news. Indeed, Rascal may prove useful to us yet. And who knows? He may very well turn out to be the best hunter we get from this litter."

Timothy cleared his throat, looking askance down at Colin. Unsure, at first, what his friend wished to convey, it eventually struck him. He had failed to stand upon Abigail's entrance! Jumping from his chair as though the seat had been afire, he stammered, "F-forgive me, Miss Newell," Colin said, stumbling over his words in his rush of embarrassment. "I seem to have left my manners in my room this evening."

"Perhaps that is a better place for them, my lord." Abigail's eyes sparkled with suppressed mirth, apparently not offended in the least. "I must admit, it is quite amusing seeing you fall all over yourself on my account. We must try to repeat the experience in future. In any case, I have never enjoyed standing upon ceremony."

Colin's brow furrowed further. Abigail was behaving as she used to, when they were young. His heart panged with the longing to hold her and he fisted his fingers to keep from reaching out.

"My old governess would have boxed your ears had you made such a confession within her hearing." Eliza laughed. "She was quite a stickler for manners and decorum, as I assume most in her position to be. Did you find it so with your own governesses, Miss Newell?"

Thank you, Eliza!

Already she was doing what he had asked. Any information, true or false, was better than none, which is what he was basically working off of currently.

The woman's smile barely faltered, yet the light left her eyes. "I cannot claim much experience."

The change in Abigail's demeanor led Colin to believe that would be the end to her ingenuous behavior. Now she would be on her guard. And, if Colin did not miss the mark, she was currently lying.

"Do you have experience with kinder governesses, Miss Newell?" Colin asked. "Or, perhaps, you meant to imply your lack of experience with polite society?"

"Colin!" Timothy snapped. "I must apologize for my friend, Miss Newell. His mouth has run away with him.

I know him to be a good man regardless of the display he seems intent on showing you tonight."

Colin burned with frustration. He had not intended to slight the woman, simply to draw her out. Yet seeing the shocked faces of all around him, he knew he had pushed too hard.

"Once more I must beg your forgiveness, Miss Newell," he answered. "Indeed, I meant no offense."

From the doorway, the butler announced dinner. The company being intimate, Timothy offered to escort his wife. Colin approached Abigail and stretched out his own arm in invitation. All eyes turned to Miss Newell, waiting to see if she would accept. Colin braced himself for the rejection—for who would blame her at this point? Colin's eyes met hers as she stood undecided.

A polite smile spread slowly across Abigail's face as she placed a hand on Colin's arm to everyone's obvious relief. Did she realize she was the very center of everyone's attention?

Even with the implied forgiveness, dinner was a silent affair. Unable to speak for the rest of the party, Colin found himself at a loss as to which topics of conversation might be safely explored, and therefore remained quiet, unable to trust his own judgement. He was infinitely grateful when the uncomfortable evening came to an end, and he was able to retire to his bedchamber.

After his disastrous interactions last evening, Colin had hidden himself away while he considered how to proceed. He had avoided seeing anyone through the whole of the day, rising early so as not to encounter anyone in the breakfast room, followed by an extensive ride through the grounds. He no longer wished to participate in Abigail's farce, yet he feared confronting her directly would lead to her disappearing once more.

Upon his return from his ride, well after luncheon would have been cleared away, he entered the library, reading title after title as he perused the shelves in the hopes that something would spark his interest. Midway through the fourth shelf, a soft snore drew his attention.

Turning from the shelves, he examined the room to find Abigail curled up on the window seat, fast asleep. Partially hidden behind the heavy brocade drapes, she had been easily overlooked when he first entered the room. Curiosity propelled him forward until he stood a mere foot away from the woman. She lay on her side, facing the room at large, with a book she had evidently been reading lying face down on the floor below her. Taking the opportunity to examine her, he noted once more the gauntness of her cheeks and the slight pallor of her skin. Yet more striking than that was the expression on her face. Unlike the peaceful oblivion generally witnessed with those lost in dreams, Abigail looked anything but at peace. Her eyes were tightly closed as if blocking out some unsightly nightmare. White lips trembled with an unspoken sob.

Colin felt a small piece of his heart break in response to the vision before him. Ere he knew what he was about he found himself kneeling before her, grasping her hand where it lay on the cushion. Cold, bony fingers clutched his and he thought she would wake with the touch. Instead, her brow smoothed, and her tension seemed to dissipate with a quiet sigh. As he picked up the book to prevent any further pages getting bent, Abigail shifted slightly.

"Colin," she moaned as she slept, her voice a ghost from his dreams. "It's a secret." Her whisper carried scenes from the past.

Droplets of sea water chilled Colin's face and hands as he ran near the lapping water. Exhilarated, he picked up his pace until he fairly flew across the wet sand. When at last he could run no more, he collapsed to the ground. Gasping, he laughed stiltedly, intoxicated with the thrill of the adventure.

A whisper arose nearby. "What are you doing?"

Colin scrambled to his feet, sand flying in all directions. Searching for the source of the question he squinted into the shadows of the night, the moon offering scant light. "Who is there? What are you doing on my land?" he demanded, hoping he sounded braver than he felt.

A high-pitched laugh sounded. "Your land? Truly?"

Relief flooded as he registered the voice of another child. Curiosity replaced his unease and he asked the shadow, "Who are you?"

He heard a rustle as a girl he guessed to be about twelve years of age stepped from the blackness into the only slightly lighter darkness near him.

"I am no one," the child stated, waving her arms around in an odd sort of dance. "I am nothing. A phantom of the night, a horrible dream." Stopping, she faced him and added sadly, "One you will likely forget on the morrow."

She spoke as one older than she appeared, as if she had lived an entire lifetime in her few short years, and Colin was grateful for the darkness that hid his confusion.

"Where did you come from? You ought not to be out of doors at this time of night. It is not safe."

A giggle. "You are here. I am hardly alone."

What sort of logic was that? "You were alone before I came. And you do not know me, we are strangers. Perhaps I have come to hurt you."

The girl stepped closer, head raised appraisingly, hands at her hips. Colin held his ground even as his heart raced, a sensation unrelated to his recent run as he took in her comely features, something he had only recently begun to notice in girls.

"You say this is your land, yet you cannot be more than a few years my senior," she reasoned. "You are too young to be the Viscount of Haverford, so I must assume you to be his son. In which case I will ask you once more, what are you doing? For I am certain you are not out, alone, in the midst of the night by permission. No lord worth his salt would allow his only son and heir to roam about unguarded at such an hour." Her head cocked to the side. "I wonder what the good viscount would say about this situation were he to catch wind of it."

Colin stretched to his full height, hoping that he could intimidate this impudent girl. Lowering his voice as much as he could, he asked, "Are you threatening me?"

Again, the girl laughed, all animosity leaving her stance. "No. I would not dare, my lord."

"You have me at a disadvantage," he said, repeating what he had heard his father say in the past, "for you have deduced who I am, yet have not given me your name."

Once again she laughed, this time bringing a slight smile to Colin's lips as well. How could one as infuriating as she have such a contagious laugh?

"I am Abigail."

Understanding dawned. "The new steward's daughter?"

"The very same," she bowed, the gesture perfectly boyish, another oddity.

"Well, Miss Abigail, to answer your question, I was running."

"I could see that you were running, but why were you running?" she pressed.

Colin turned to face the sea. "I have always dreamed of running along the beach at night. Tonight, I decided to do it."

"And what does your father think of you being out, alone, at night?" she said, repeating her earlier observation.

He turned back to Abigail. "As I am certain you have guessed, he does not know. I would ask that you keep this between us."

"I will make a deal with you. I will keep your clandestine activities secret, if you will do the same for me."

"What are you doing out, anyway?"

She leaned closer and whispered, "It's a secret."

Coming back to himself, he gave her hand a gentle squeeze. What experiences she must have had since the night they had parted for her to suffer such horrors in her sleep. As gently as he could, he arranged himself on the bench near her head. If holding her hand brought her the peace to rest, he would gladly sit near her always.

Chapter 7

Thoughts of Colin swirled through Abigail's mind as she roused from slumber. Never in recent memory could she remember basking in such sweet contentment. Her stomach rumbled with unyielding hunger, yet she was loath to stir as the action might expunge the sense of serenity currently encompassing her.

Slowly, she became aware of a rubbing sensation on her hand, a slow and smooth circular motion. Warmth infused the area and she clung tighter, willing her eyes to remain closed. Colin's face floated before her, as clear as ever as she imagined him holding her hand, wrapping her in the safety of his arms, protecting her from the ugliness of the world, and her dreams.

The slight rustle of a person adjusting in the seat next to her brought her back to full consciousness. The rubbing stopped. Opening one eye a mere slit, she peeked around, careful not to move.

"I know you are awake, so you may as well sit up," a familiar voice said from beside her.

Startled, and irritated at her failure, she took a fortifying breath, attempting to calm her racing heart. Colin sat next to her on the window seat where she had been reading before she had evidently dozed off. Her book now resided in his lap.

Has he been reading it while I slept?

How long she had slept she could not say, although the hour appeared much later than before as shadows leapt through the room in time with the dancing flames of candles. A quick glance out the window showed the sun had set and the world was settling into darkness.

"How late is it?" she asked, shifting to a sitting position and pulling her hand out of his. Smoothing the wrinkles from her dress as best she could, she avoided looking at Colin directly. "It must be nearly time to dress for dinner."

"It is nearing seven, I believe," he confirmed.

She had been laying here for over three hours. Stretching her stiff muscles, she attempted to recall the last time she had slept so peacefully. How much of that time had Colin been present?

Turning to face him for the first time she noted his countenance. His expression was softer than she had ever seen it, drinking her in as if she might disappear at any moment.

Suddenly, she knew.

Her charade was over. He knew who she was. There could be no pretense now. She had failed. The surety with which that thought struck her rivaled any physical attack her father had ever rained down on her.

Thoughts, tumbling over themselves, ran through her mind in a mere moment. What could she say? There was nothing that would justify her presence in this house, with these people. Colin and his friends who were so far above her in status, and in character. She did not belong with good people, as she was far from good herself.

She ought to leave, but to go where? Her father would certainly not welcome her back, and with no friends outside of these walls she truly had nowhere to go. Would Eliza cast her out in the dead of night? Or would she be allowed to wait until morning?

Either way, it was time to pack her things.

Standing, she mumbled, "I should go."

Colin grasped her hand once more, forcing her to remain.

"You think," Colin said, his voice raspy with some emotion Abigail could not name, "after ten excruciatingly long years of searching for you that I would merely sit here and watch you walk away?" He rose and turned her to face him. "Am I not even to be afforded a word?"

He has been looking for me?

All that time, when she thought he must have forgotten her, he had been searching. She looked up into his stormy grey eyes, their color so like her own that it was like being reunited with something she had lost ago. "What is there to say? I—"

Before she could formulate even a fleeting thought, Colin's mouth crushed down on hers and she was caught up in his arms. All thoughts fled as she reacted with every ounce of strength she had. Colin was greedy, hungry for her in a way she had never experienced before, and yet her body responded in kind. She gripped the back of his neck, willing him to never leave her, to save her from the hell she knew without him. Her senses exploded with him; his scent, his taste, his radiating warmth. She thought she would never get enough.

Eventually, the frenzy died down, and she unwillingly returned to the present. Hope replaced the despair of a few moments earlier. Colin had loved her once, perhaps he could love her again. Given his response to her just now that seemed like a distinct possibility. Yet hope had failed her in the past, and it was difficult to trust in now.

Abigail stroked his cheek, wishing to hold onto the moment, yet knowing it could not last. “I suppose we ought to...”

“Shh, not yet,” he whispered breathlessly, pressing his forehead to hers and closing his eyes. “Give me a moment.”

She waited a heartbeat, then two and three as he took breath after breath. Finally she pulled back from his embrace and tried once more, glancing at the wide-open doorway. “Colin, I—”

“Why did you not say something?” he interrupted, his voice rising as anger began to take over. Those hands that had held her so ensnared a moment before now pushed her gently away, as if he was afraid to continue touching her. “How could you stand in front of me and not tell me who you were?”

Abigail’s own ire flared, and she turned it back on him as she folded her arms over her chest. “How could you have not known me? I knew you at first glance, immediately upon your arrival. Was I so easily forgotten?”

“Forgotten?” he croaked, running both hands through his hair and pacing away from her. “If only heaven had allowed me to forget. Every day I searched for you! Every resource I had was spent scouring the country for you! I am only here now because Bow Street led me here, and I arrive to find you as the honored guest of my closest friends. Yet you stood there and acted as if we had never met!" Turning his back on her, he rested with both hands leaning on the mantel, head lowered.

Sympathy filled her. Was it truly possible that he had suffered from her absence? That he had longed for her as she had longed for him? The idea was nearly more than she could fathom.

"Colin, I—"

"Where is he?" Colin demanded, interrupting once more. Rounding on her, he grasped her arms, eyes wild.

"What?" Her still somewhat foggy mind raced trying to keep pace with him.

"Your father, the cur," he spat. "Where is he?"

Her father? Was that why he had searched for her all this time? Simply to find her father? Of course he would wish to recover what her father had stolen from his family all those years ago. How could she have not thought of this possibility? Never had it occurred to her that once she was reunited with the man she loved he would only care for what had transpired in the past. And none of that was her fault! Did he blame her for the sins of her father?

"I-I do not know," she answered truthfully. Her father never deigned to inform her of his plans, giving her only the barest amount of information. They were to meet in a fortnight at the Royal Arms Inn just outside of London, but his current whereabouts was anyone's guess. Her only link with him had been the notes she left for him in the meadow, where she had nearly been caught out by Colin the previous day. And it was her guess that he was not fetching those himself. He always seemed to have men willing to run that sort of errand for him.

Colin's countenance cleared as he took a calming breath. "Good. That's good." His eyes returned to hers and she saw the tempest that raged within begin to calm as a slow smile crept up. "I simply cannot fathom how you are here." His hands loosened their grip on her arms as he leaned his forehead against hers once more.

Had she heard him correctly? Was it truly good that her father was nowhere nearby? Hope flashed once more as she stood immobile, unwilling to pull away from him. If she was wrong, she would at least have this one moment with him to remember.

The silence of the night encased them as they stood, breathing the same air for what felt like the first time in ages. The ticking of the clock and the crackling of the fire the only disruptions to the utter peace that Colin's presence brought. At least until her stomach rumbled once more and her hunger returned full-force.

Abigail's mortification grew as Colin chuckled and she finally pushed away from him as her face heated.

"I suppose you would be famished after such a day as this," he teased.

"Yes, well, who was it that allowed me to waste away the time?" she countered.

"Waste the time? Dear Abigail, you appeared to be in desperate need of a decent rest." His eyes raked over her causing her to cross her arms in a self-conscious gesture. Yet instead of the lustful leering she had endured from her father's friends over the years, Colin's eyes held only concern. "Aside from being hungry, are you well? Truly well?"

"Truthfully, I am better now than I have been in ages," she replied with a shy smile. Hope was a wonderful thing, yet came with its own amount of fear. She knew better than to think that happiness could last, and already worries of what would become of her once Colin made her identity known to his friends began to trickle through.

"Hm," Colin breathed with a frown, clearly unsatisfied with her response. Did he not believe her? How she wished she knew Colin as well now as she once had. "You do appear to have a little more color after your nap just now. Or is it something unrelated to sleep that has your cheeks flushed?"

Oh! The man was unrepentant in his observations, and he knew her all too well. Defensively, she responded, "All I know is that I do not sleep well, at least aside from the phenomenal nap I took just now, and I do not have much of an appetite. Although, I currently find myself to be quite famished."

"Right." He nodded. "Well, one thing is for certain..." he added with a grin.

Set at ease by his rapid return to good humor, she asked, "And what is that?"

Taking her hand, and guiding her upstairs where they would both prepare for dinner, he laughed. "There will be plenty of conversation with dinner tonight."

With that they parted ways for their respective chambers. Abigail felt more weighed down with insecurities with each step Colin took away from her.

Molly prattled on while helping Abigail dress for dinner, yet Abigail's thoughts ran wild. Colin had not thrown her out. He had embraced her, kissed her even! The memory of their kiss made her lips tingle once more and she fought to push all other cares from her mind. She barely registered the knock on her door before Molly opened it. After speaking with the visitor for a moment, Molly closed the door once more and returned to her work.

"Dinner will be a bit delayed, miss. The lord and lady have only now returned from Whitegarden Manor and require a few more minutes to dress."

Abigail stood. "I believe I shall wait for them in the drawing room." If she was lucky Colin would soon join her. Such company would be infinitely more enjoyable than waiting here as the maid finished her work of clearing away the remains of the afternoon.

"Very well, miss." Molly bobbed a quick curtsy and continued with her work.

Crossing the threshold into the corridor, Abigail closed the door behind her. Suddenly a hand clamped down over her mouth and nose, muffling the scream that rose in her throat. She was yanked back against a body, hard and unyielding, dragged down the hallway away from her door and the safety that Molly might bring. Her hands flew up in a vain attempt to tear the hand that held her bound away from her face even as an arm grasped her around her midsection, sufficiently pinning her in place. She fleetingly noticed that the candles at this end of the corridor had been extinguished.

"Now, now, Abby," a male voice whispered in her ear. "Jes' stay calm and ye won't be hurt."

Bile rose in her throat as the smell of stale ale and what she assumed to have been yesterday's lunch wafted over her. She knew from previous experiences that struggling in such a circumstance was largely futile. She forced herself to still, focusing only on filling her lungs with air, a difficult task as the man's hand remained over her nose.

"Good, very good," he said. "I knowed ye was a smart one. Smart 'nough to not scream, too. You wouldn't want no one else gettin' hurt, and worse'n what I can do to ye, with yer father given you his protection."

Protection?

Her father had never protected her. Bringing her up in such a life, to become such a person as he. Yet, now she was afforded no time to contemplate as the hand gripping her abdomen began to rove. Abigail fought down her panic. Becoming hysterical would not help her in this situation. As much as she longed to have Molly, Colin, or anyone to come to her rescue, she knew the truth in this man's words. She could not put these good people in such danger. She nodded her head slightly to affirm she would not scream.

Taking his hand from her mouth, yet keeping his arms around her so she could not turn and face him, he said,

"Now, I come with a warnin' from yer dear papa. Be sure you 'member what yer about, and don't go gettin' any ideas."

Pushing Abigail roughly to the floor, the man rushed to the end of the corridor, around a corner leading to the servants' stairs. Gasping for air, she rolled into a sitting position. She briefly considered calling out for help, now that her mouth was no longer obstructed, but decided against it. Raising the alarm about an intruder would invite questions about what he had been after and she could not tell anyone he had been here to warn her.

Why would her father have sent such a message? Did he not trust her to accomplish her task? And who was the man who had accosted her? She had not gotten a look at his face, so she would be unable to identify him. Was this an isolated visit from him, or was he perhaps a servant within the household whom her father was paying to keep an eye on her?

She brushed the tears from her cheeks. Using the wall as support, she stood, noticing the wrinkles now apparent in her gown. As excited as she had previously been about spending the evening with Colin, she realized she was now in no fit state to go down to dinner. Thankfully, Molly was still in her room and could help clean her up.

"Is something the matter, miss?" Molly asked with concern, taking in Abigail's disheveled appearance upon her return. "What on earth?"

Abigail took the maid's outstretched hands as support and allowed herself to be guided to a chair. "I have been rather clumsy, I'm afraid. I slipped on the hem of this gown," she shook the skirt out as if aggravated with it, "and took a tumble. This dress has always been a tad long, and I have meant to hem it. This is the fruit of procrastination, Molly. Will you help straighten me up once more before I go down?"

"Of course, miss. Don't you worry about a thing. We will have you fixed up in no time, and I will fix the dress tomorrow, if you like. It would be no bother."

Not wishing to add to the poor maid's workload because of a lie, Abigail quickly shook her head. "There is no need. I am perfectly capable of fixing it myself. If you could help me now, that will be sufficient."

Once Abigail had assured Molly that she was unhurt, Molly was as good as her word, fixing Abigail up as if nothing had gone amiss. And as Molly went on about the merits of her herbal remedies, Abigail considered her options, yet there was really only one. Her encounter with the man in the corridor only served to solidify her previous knowledge. She would never be free of her father. Regardless of Colin's presence, or the safety Abigail felt when he was near, he was no match for her father. Christopher Wallace was not a man to be trifled with, nor a man one wished to anger. He was clever, elusive and brutal. If she failed him he would certainly track her down and the punishment would be… Even now she could scarcely think of it.

And what of Colin? If it were discovered that she was involved with him aside from both being guests here, he would also be made to suffer, or worse. The ramifications did not bear thinking of.

Her search for the jewels must continue. On the morrow she would attempt to search the Marchioness's chamber. Tonight she would fall asleep formulating a plan that would allow her access.

She simply could not fail.

Chapter 8

Colin's grin remained firmly locked in place as he finished tying his cravat. Thankfully, he knew how to do such a thing, as his valet, Morley, was needed for a more important task. Upon realizing Abigail was here, Colin had sent the man as his proxy back to Somerset on a vital errand. He had been instructed that speed was of the essence, and expected the man to return in a mere matter of days. Until such time, however, Colin must care for himself somewhat.

Tonight he was content to complete his preparations on his own as he contemplated the miracle of his kiss with Abigail. He knew it had been wrong of him to take such liberties, yet he had been as a man possessed. Sitting so near her for hours, caressing her hand in his, her visage of complete peace, had made him feel grounded for what seemed the first time in his life. The numerous years of longing had finally burst forth, and he could not regret it.

He would not take advantage of her again, however. Now that she was back in his life, he would make certain that she never left again. At least, not permanently. He would head out in the morning in search of a clergyman to issue a marriage license. What he had desired most his entire adult life was about to be his.

Of course, there was still the issue of asking Abigail to be his bride. A small thing, really, considering he had found her at last. And her response to his kiss left him with no doubt that she cared for him still.

This day had played out in his head so many times, yet he had never imagined how absolutely giddy he would be over her return.

With a carefree swing in his step Colin made his way to the drawing room. At the door he was met by a footman with a message that dinner would be delayed a quarter hour as Eliza and Timothy had been delayed in town and had only recently returned.

No matter. It would allow time for Colin to decide how to share the happy news that the secret of Abigail's identity was no more, and all could be spoken of freely. There seemed to still be plenty of secrets surrounding Abigail, yet her identity need not be one of them.

Once in the room, he found it impossible to sit down. His body fairly shook with pent-up energy. Rubbing his hands together, he paced the room, grateful it was quite large with plenty of room to move about. Fortunately, he did not have to wait long before Abigail joined him.

One look at her told him all was not right and he deflated instantly. As he watched, her eyes darted from one end of the room to the other, her hands twisting tightly together. She barely glanced at him and dipped a small curtsy before moving to the chair furthest away and settling on the edge of the seat. The image of a frightened bird came to mind as he watched her, afraid that one wrong word would send her flying away. He must find a way to put her at ease, yet without knowing the cause of her distress he had no clear view on how to proceed.

"Abigail," he began gently, taking a small step toward her.

Her gaze locked with his, yet she remained silent.

Another step toward her and she shrunk back slightly. Very well, he would stay where he was, as hard as it proved for him to do so when every instinct told him to protect her. At least it placed him between her and the door so as to make her escape impossible, should she attempt it. Not that he would ever consider keeping her captive against her will. He hoped it would never come to that.

"Has something happened?" he asked hesitantly.

The candlelight reflected off the tears that filled her eyes before she blinked, and the moment ended. He watched in fascination as her countenance shifted. Suddenly it was as if a stranger sat before him.

"I am quite well, Colin," she said smoothly, absolutely no quaver to be heard.

"I am relieved to hear that," Eliza said from behind Colin, having entered the room unnoticed, on the arm of her husband. With their arrival, Colin had no choice but to set aside his concern.

"Yes," Abigail stated, her gaze turning to the newcomers. "I am certain I have your gracious hospitality to thank for it, Lady Bedford. Yours as well, my lord."

"No thanks are necessary," Eliza said with a wave of her hand. "And I really must insist upon being addressed as Eliza. As much as I love my husband, I am still quite unused to being referred to as Lady Bedford. It makes me feel quite matronly, in fact."

"One thing you are not, my dear," Timothy said, consoling her, "is matronly."

The gaze shared between Timothy and Eliza seemed to make the temperature in the drawing room rise a degree or two. Were all recently wedded couples this unbelievably happy? Doubtful, though it was a fate that Colin aspired to nonetheless.

Giggling softly, Eliza broke their eye contact and turned back to her guests. "I must apologize for abandoning you this afternoon. I was needed at the hospital once more. I trust you spent your time pleasantly?" she asked, directing her question to Colin.

"Yes, quite," he answered for them both, then cleared his throat. "In point of fact, I have some news to share this evening." Adopting a formal stance he placed one hand behind his back. "Lord and Lady Bedford, allow me to present to you," he paused briefly for effect, "Miss Abigail Wallace." Making a show of it he swept his arm out in a broad gesture towards Abigail, fighting a grin at the foolishness of it, yet determined to draw a smile from her.

Abigail's face flamed adorably, and Colin relished the moment. Timothy and Eliza's faces both registered confusion as his words sank in, doubtless thinking on Colin's insistence of secrecy.

The couple shared another glance as Eliza took a seat, the marquess remaining behind her, hands on her shoulders.

Eliza's brows furrowed. "Well, I believe I speak for my husband as well as myself when I say we are speechless. This is quite a pronouncement."

"Indeed," Timothy agreed. "We seem to have missed quite the afternoon, my dear. Perhaps Colin could share how this all came about?"

Before Colin could respond, Ridley cleared his throat from the doorway and announced dinner.

"As much as I hate to say it, further explanation will have to wait until after we are seated," Timothy replied, then beckoned to his wife with an outstretched arm. "Come, my dear."

The short walk to the dining room was painfully silent, and he had never seen Abigail appear so stiff, as if the very tension he felt was holding her hostage as well.

Scarcely had the first course been served than Eliza's gaze sought Abigail's. "Why were you introduced to me as Miss Newell? And why did you never correct the error?"

Silence reigned as all eyes once again landed on Abigail. Watching her hands twisting and her eyes darting between those gathered, Colin once more got the impression that she wished to flee. As they were seated across from one another, it was impossible for him to lend support with a pat of the hand or a gentle nudge. He hoped to catch her eye, but her glance refused to settle on him for more than a mere moment.

Timothy, seeming to realize Abigail's reticence, attempted to help her along. "I know a bit of your story as Colin has spoken of you from time to time, yet I do not believe my wife knows much of it. Why don't you start at the beginning?"

Abigail blinked, once more erasing all emotion from her countenance.

How does she do that?

A quick breath, and then she began. "My name is Abigail, that much is true. At one time, my father worked as steward for Colin's, I mean Lord Haverford's, father."

"Come, Abigail," Colin protested. "For heaven's sake use my Christian name."

Abigail's lips rose in the semblance of a smile. "Colin and I met when I was twelve years old." She went on to describe their relationship, their nightly meetings, away from other people. Colin was gratified to learn of her anticipation for his visits from Eton, to know she had looked forward to them as much as he had.

She spoke only briefly of her father and his work on the estate. Colin waited for her to speak of Christopher's abuses to her, yet she said nothing of them. Colin himself would never forget the bruises he had been able to discern even in the moonlight, her flesh tender beneath his touch as he embraced her. Even now, years later, he grew hot thinking of it. What sort of man could raise his fist to a child, not once, but time and time again? After all this time Colin still could not comprehend the cruelty.

The tale was interrupted only by the changing courses of the meal as Abigail took scarcely a bite of anything placed before her. Thinking back, he had scarcely seen her take five bites together since his arrival at Edgemont.

"Then why were you introduced to me as Abigail Newell?" Eliza asked once more, drawing Colin out of his private thoughts.

Abigail hesitated, looking to Colin for the first time since her tale began. He nodded his support, adding a small smile for good measure, and wishing he could do more to assist her.

Abigail, seeming to realize her moment of weakness, shifted her eyes once more back to Eliza. "My father is not the most honorable of men. About six months back I decided to sever all ties with him. A friend of mine helped me travel to London where I procured work as a governess. I began going by the name Newell in the hopes that it would make it impossible for my father to find me."

"Why did you not come to me?" Colin asked softly, attempting to keep any trace of hurt from his voice.

“I did not wish to be a burden.” Her head lowered, but not before Colin glimpsed the tears forming in her eyes. How he longed to pull her into his arms, to comfort her, yet they were not alone.

Raising her head she turned back to the others, eyes dry once more, yet strangely unfocused. “It was not long before I was found, however. I am uncertain how he found me.” Her gaze locked with Colin’s once more. “He sees everything, knows everything. That is when I met Eliza.”

Eliza gasped with some realization Colin did not understand. Looking back to Abigail, he saw her agitation, visible through the jerkiness of her movements. She pushed her chair from the table and rose, pacing behind the chairs. “He will always find me,” she muttered. “I can never be free.”

On his feet in an instant, forgetting decorum as well as all manners accepted within polite society, Colin moved around the table and grasped her hands, halting her movements. “I believe that is enough explanation for this evening.”

“Of course,” Timothy agreed. “Miss...,” he hesitated. “My goodness, what are we to call you?”

“If you approve, I would prefer Newell,” she answered. “I do not wish to cause the servants any confusion.”

"Yes, of course. You are welcome to stay for as long as it takes us to sort this out." Timothy turned back to his wife. "Come, my dear. Let us retire." Taking his wife's hand, he escorted her out, paying no heed to their unfinished meal. He carefully left the door open so as to avoid impropriety. Having departed so far from appropriate behavior, Colin could see no reason to stand on any remaining ceremony. After escorting Abigail to the drawing room, he guided her to the settee. Colin ran a hand through his hair as he paced away from her.

"I know you are blaming yourself, Colin, and you must stop." Abigail's words, meant to calm him, hit their mark.

"Even after all of these years, you still know me so well."

She laughed, full and genuine. "You are not a difficult person to make out, you never have been. You show your emotions for all to see."

"Does your father know you are here?" he asked, changing the course of conversation.

Abigail's eyes twitched and she bit her lip. Colin knew her well too, and was aware when she was lying.

"No. I have not seen him since he left me at the hospital in London."

Why would she lie? Would he truly need to regain her trust after all this time? If so, that was something he was perfectly willing to do. Perhaps in time she would confide in him. And then realization finally hit Colin, as it must have found Eliza a few moments earlier. "He put you there, in the hospital." It was not a question, a simple statement he knew to be true.

In lieu of continuing that conversation, Abigail asked, "Do you recall when we found that dinghy and we took it out on the pond every night for a week?"

Laughing, he turned back to her. "I slept for hours each afternoon. My mother sent for Doctor Hursch, convinced I had picked up some disease from school and that I would contaminate the entire household."

Abigail gazed at him in shock. "You never told me." Her laughter drove all thoughts of her deceit from his head. They remained laughing over reminiscences for another quarter hour before Colin insisted they retire. As loath as he was to be parted from her so soon after being reunited, seeing the dark circles return under her eyes reminded him that she still needed rest. And above all else, he would do what was best for her.

Chapter 9

Abigail slowly peered out from behind a floor-length tapestry where she had been hiding for the past twenty minutes. Would Eliza's lady's maid ever finish her work and leave the lady's bedchamber? Eliza had gone down to breakfast ages ago, and if her maid would simply leave the room, Abigail would have a few minutes to search it. Abigail herself had sent for a tray this morning. After the events of the day before, no one could blame her for not appearing. Her absence from the breakfast room would not be suspicious.

Waiting was the worst part, as it left her too much time to think. And of all the things she ought to be thinking of, one clearly dominated, bringing a fleeting smile to her lips.

Colin.

Their kiss.

Even now his words echoed within her. *Every day I searched for you...Every resource I had was spent scouring the country...*

Was that not love? The sort of abiding affection that lasted through the years and would never fade away? Dreams were built upon such foundations. And yet, just when she had resolved to rush back to Colin's arms and bask in the safety he offered, something held her back.

Father...and his spies.

How he had managed to infiltrate the marquess's estate was anyone's guess. It managed to further solidify what she already knew—nowhere was safe. Father always did keep most of his associates away from her. As much as she used to hope it was a way to protect her, it occurred to her now that it was likely to protect himself. If she were to go to the authorities, she would have precious little valuable information to use against him, and even less to use against those he worked with. He was quite brilliant, really, keeping the important details of his dealings secret even from his own daughter.

A click sounded from down the hall and Abigail held her breath as she peeked out once more. Her waiting had paid off. She watched as the maid exited the room and walked toward the servant staircase at the other end of the corridor, paying no heed to the bulge behind this particular tapestry.

Even with the path before her clear, Abigail's heart threatened to beat its way out of her chest. Her feet refused to move and she broke out in a cold sweat. What was wrong with her? Never before had she experienced any of these symptoms before she performed a task. Her guilt typically invaded after it was done, not before.

Why was she still standing hidden behind the tapestry? The jewels her father was so intent upon having, were bound to be within Eliza's dressing room unguarded, now that her maid had left. This was Abigail's chance.

Think of something else, she told herself. *Take no thought as to what will happen to you if you are caught.*

Caught or not, what was the difference? If found, she would be cast out, likely sent before a magistrate and charged with her crimes. Destined to spend the rest of her days in Newgate. A shiver ran down Abigail's spine at the thought of that place, the place her father had used to terrorize her when she was little. Tales of the rats, the filth, and the other prisoners so desperate for any human contact that they would break themselves for a chance to go to the infirmary. These thoughts still haunted her dreams to this day.

Yet if she failed, would her fate not be worse?

Either way, Abigail lost. Then why do something she was morally opposed to?

Abigail straightened with resolve. She would *not* be entering the Marchioness's bedchamber, nor would she continue any other clandestine activity. Instead, she would go down to breakfast and then she would spend whatever time she could with Colin before her luck ran out and she was forced away from him once more.

Boldly, she thrust aside the tapestry and purposefully set off for the breakfast room. She would enjoy this time with Colin. As it was certain to be her last moments of happiness in life, she would not squander them.

Eliza smiled above her food as Abigail entered the breakfast room. "I trust you slept well."

"I did, thank you," Abigail said, forcing herself to be brave and meet Eliza's friendly eyes and smile in return. "In truth, I feel more rested than I have in years." She smiled as she realized the truthfulness of her words.

"I am glad to hear it, although I doubt I can claim any responsibility. It is likely all due to being reunited with an old friend."

Heat flooded Abigail's face, unable to deny the assumption. For she, too, credited Colin's presence to her improved state of mind, that and her recent resolve. The fog she had lived under for so long was clearing, and she could finally breathe.

"With my spending so much time of late with the doctor assisting him with his rounds of the neighborhood, I find myself quite behind in the duties of running this household," Eliza went on as Abigail filled a charger and joined her at the table. "Particularly in regards to the dinner party this evening. All of our recent excitement had put this evening quite out of my head. I do hope you will not overly mind entertaining yourself once more this morning so I may see to the final preparations?"

"Not at all." Abigail was quick to assure. "I have been hoping for another opportunity to check in on Rascal, and to further explore the grounds."

"Another day I shall have to join you. I do love to be out of doors."

"I should like that very much," Abigail said truthfully, thinking once more on the novelty of having another true friend.

"My mother and sisters shall be returning from their travels today and ought to arrive sometime this afternoon."

"I am eager to meet them."

Eliza took a final bite of her coddled eggs and placed her fork down. A footman who had been standing nearby quickly moved to pull her chair back for her.

"There will be plenty of introductions this evening," Eliza continued as she stood and moved to the doorway. "I do hope they do not become too tedious. Since I have so recently come out of mourning, this shall be my first chance to host a gathering with the local gentry as many of them I have yet to meet. I confess, it was rather pleasant not being required to entertain since my marriage to Timothy. Although, there is an end to all things, and now it is time to move on."

"May I be of any help to you, Eliza?

Eliza waved her offer away. "I thank you, but one of us ought to enjoy this day, rather than be confined to the house finalizing preparations."

After Eliza's departure, Abigail ate a few more bites as she wondered where Colin would be at this time of day. She ought to have asked Eliza, yet she had missed her opportunity.

Once finished and quite satisfied, she glanced at her empty plate. She could not remember the last time she had been able to eat so much.

Deciding to take advantage of her renewed energy, she made her way to the rear of the estate toward the stables. She was eager to check on the progress of the tiny pup. Eliza had been thoughtful in providing Abigail with frequent updates, but it would do Abigail good to see for herself.

In truth, she was also fascinated with horses, never having been afforded the opportunity to learn to ride in her youth, yet always in awe of their brute strength and agile beauty. Any excuse to watch those majestic animals must be taken advantage of.

Perhaps Colin would teach her to ride...

Such a thing could never be, she thought with a shake of her head. She would never be allowed the time it would take for her to learn. Her father was not a patient man.

"Might I help ya, miss?"

The question took her by surprise, so deep had she been within her own head, she had failed to notice the boy approach. She recognized him as the boy who had been at Eliza's bidding the morning the pups were born. He could not be more than ten, though she could see him rising on his toes in a vain attempt to appear taller.

"Possibly," she answered. A quick glance behind him at a horse tethered to a stake in the middle of the paddock gave her an idea. "Is that one of Lord Bedford's horses?" she asked. Although the answer was obvious, it never hurt to play the ignorant young miss.

The lad rewarded her with a grin. "Aye, miss. The master likes his fine 'orses. Right particular 'bout their training, 'e is." His chest puffed up.

"And are you involved with their training?" she asked, walking with him to the fence enclosing the area where the horse currently grazed.

"Aye. I 'elp me pa, he bein' the stable master 'ere."

"You must be quite trustworthy to have such a powerful man as Lord Bedford trust you with such a task," she said solemnly.

The boy beamed as her praise hit its mark.

"I believe we ought to be introduced." She dipped into a deep curtsy. "I am Miss Abigail Newell. And you are?"

"Camden Finnian," he said, dipping into an awkward bow.

Abigail had an idea. This young boy may well be able to help her discover the identity of her father's spy. If her father had hired a man to accost her the other night, Camden may have seen him. Although, if her father had simply slipped some silver into the pocket of a current servant, it would be impossible for Abigail to ever let down her guard.

"Well, Mr. Finnian, I imagine that you see a lot of what goes on around this estate. Am I correct?"

"Aye. I reckon I see more'n 'bout anyone."

"I do not doubt it," she said solemnly. "I wonder if you have seen any strangers poking around lately."

"None what I can think of, miss. The only stranger I can thinks of is you, but you ain't a stranger now I knows your name."

"No," she said with a smile at the sweet boy, "we are no longer strangers, we are friends you and I. And as a friend, would you be willing to tell me if you do see anyone hanging around? Someone who does not belong, I mean."

"'Course, miss. Ain't nothin' 'ard 'bout that."

"No, nothing hard indeed," she agreed. A weight was lifted off her shoulders knowing that another person would be watching out for more of her father's henchmen, or her father himself. It simply felt better to know she would not be the only one keeping a wary eye out. She gave Camden another smile. "Do you think we could keep this between the two of us?"

"'Course, miss," he repeated.

"I can tell that you truly are as trustworthy as you seem, Mr. Finnian. I am quite happy to call you my friend."

Camden blushed at the praise before running off to do whatever work young boys do on such vast estates, leaving Abigail suddenly missing the company.

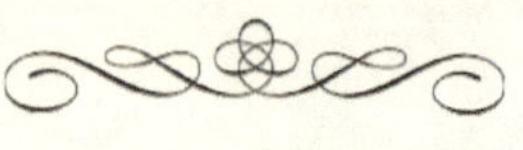

"You look lovely, miss." Molly smiled. "It is a right honor for you to be allowed to wear one of the marchioness's own gowns."

Eliza had sent several gowns to Abigail's chamber this afternoon, with the message that she would be pleased to have Abigail wear one of them this evening. Would the goodness of the marchioness never end?

Without waiting for a response Molly began gathering up the discarded garments in preparation of returning them. Abigail had been unsure as to which dress to wear, and had insisted that Molly choose as the maid had a wonderful eye. Having chosen a lovely cream-colored evening gown, the maid now laid it on the bed while seeing to Abigail's hair. The amount of pins Molly seemed determined to stick on Abigail's head seemed entirely ridiculous, yet Abigail was once more pleasantly surprised by the end result. And more than anything Abigail wished to look her best this evening. As she would scarcely know any of the other guests, she was relying on Colin's company throughout the party. She left her room as trepidation for the evening rose in her chest.

The noise from the drawing room could be heard before Abigail entered. Not having attended many functions, and not having the benefit of attending a finishing school, she was unclear as to the protocol to follow upon one's arrival. Her hope of skirting the edges of the room until she found Colin was dashed as Eliza spotted her and rushed to her side.

"Come and I will introduce you to my sisters."

Abigail felt like a wildflower in a rose garden, small and insignificant, when placed next to the beautiful women Eliza introduced her to. Her mother and sisters were every bit as gracious and welcoming as they were lovely.

"What a darling girl you have been to keep our Eliza company while we were away," Lady Gravestone said, a grateful smile on her face. "Although she is a married woman now, I was relieved to hear she would yet have some female company. Having come from a family of girls I think the solitude of this house would have worn on her if you had not come."

"I was happy for the invitation, Lady Graveston, I assure you." This truth came easily to her lips, as any time away from her father was welcomed. "Your daughter has been so good to me."

Many introductions followed as Eliza seemed bent on acquainting her with the entire county. Most faded away nearly as soon as they were uttered, yet one would not be forgotten.

"Mr. Morgan, might I introduce to you our good friend, Miss Abigail Newell." Abigail's knees shook from exhaustion as she sank into yet another curtsy. "Miss Newell, this is our friend and neighbor, Mr. Peter Morgan."

The middle-aged gentleman's face blanched as he took a good look at Abigail. For what reason, she could not guess. He quickly recovered himself and completed the requisite bow.

"Forgive me, Miss Newell," he said. "I merely find myself taken aback. For you are the very image of my sister Hannah."

Abigail stiffened. Hannah? That had been her mother's Christian name.

"How peculiar," Eliza stated, clearly interested.

"Quite," Mr. Morgan agreed, just as Ridley announced dinner, inhibiting further conversation.

Fortunately, Abigail was granted a slight reprieve from the uncomfortable encounter, as she found Colin quite suddenly at her side.

"Might I escort you in to dinner, Miss Newell?" he asked formally.

The sound of that name on his tongue yet felt foreign, as it was not the name he knew her by. Yet it had been she who had insisted upon keeping it. What a relief it would be when all such pretenses were done away. She had often dreamed of a day when she would have a name of her own, one that was truly hers and not an alias concocted by her father or herself.

The dining room they entered was one unknown to Abigail as it was only used for large gatherings. Two long tables were set some distance apart, each with place settings arranged to easily accommodate twenty or so guests. It was little wonder at the crowd of people that had been in the drawing room and the seemingly endless parade of introductions.

Colin saw her seated, giving her elbow a gentle squeeze as she sat. Abigail smiled up at him. With him near, she could weather any number of strangers and their questions. It was a blessed thing, too, since once the entire company was at last seated and the meal was underway, Abigail found her reprieve at an end.

"I wonder, Miss Newell, where are you joining us from?" Mr. Morgan asked her from across the mammoth table, drawing the attention of several other guests.

"I am lately of London, sir."

Please let that be the end of it.

Turning to Colin who had taken the seat next to her, she opened her mouth to speak, but was interrupted.

"And before that?" Mr. Morgan asked.

"She was raised near my family estate," Colin stated, "in Somerset."

Abigail was relieved by Colin's easy assistance, and Mr. Morgan looked impressed. It was the first emotion Abigail had been able to recognize from the man. He seemed inordinately curious about her. After her decision to treasure her time with Colin, she resented this stranger's attempt to wrest her attention.

"And who are your parents?" Mr. Morgan continued.

Abigail stuffed a forkful of fish into her mouth to delay her answer. She had learned years ago that when lying, it was best to remain as truthful as possible. Colin covertly patted her free hand where it rested in her lap, possibly to add his support, yet the sensation of his touch distracted her and she had to stifle a pleased smile.

"I am the daughter of Christopher and Hannah Newell."

For a man hearing fictional names of people he could not possibly know, Mr. Morgan was awfully shocked. At least, that was the impression Abigail received when he dropped his own fork and spilled his goblet of wine. As he attempted to right his misstep, the liquid quickly dripped off the table into the gentleman's lap causing him to jump from his seat.

Colin removed his hand as he and the other gentlemen around the table rose at the ruckus, some stretching to use their napkins to sop up the blood red liquid, aided by the footmen attending the dinner.

"I-I apologize," Mr. Morgan said to the room at large. In the chaos he was met by a footman who motioned first at Mr. Morgan's clothing and then to follow him. They both left the room.

Turning to Colin, Abigail raised her eyebrows in question.

"I cannot fathom," Colin answered, as if she had fully asked a question. He retook his seat. "I have met Mr. Morgan on a number of occasions, yet I never witnessed him make such a fool of himself. It is quite curious."

Chapter 10

It is strange how quickly one's life can be transformed. Something as simple as a few words jotted down on parchment can alter the course of one's life forever. Abigail did not give one thought to the messages delivered to the breakfast room the following morning, until Eliza spoke.

"You must have made quite the impression on Mr. Morgan," she said to Abigail, placing the paper she had been reading down beside her plate. She scanned the rest of the party which included the marquess, Colin, and Eliza's family who would be staying at Edgemont until they all traveled back to London for the Season. "We have all been invited for tea this afternoon. He would like us to view the portrait of his sister, the one he mentioned you remind him of."

"I am surprised he would draw such attention to it," Timothy mused.

"What do you mean?" Colin asked between bites of toast.

"From what I recall, his sister disappeared before I was born. It was quite the scandal at the time as it was believed she ran off with an undeserving young man. As far as I know, the Morgans have not spoken of her since. Peter was her only sibling and luckily his reputation was able to recover from such an unsavory association. My mother had been close friends with his sister and was devastated by her loss. Fortunately, my mother was already betrothed to my father at the time and she had support to see her through her loss."

"That poor family," Lady Gravestone sighed. "They must have been heartbroken."

"Perhaps," Timothy allowed.

"Not all families have strong emotional ties with one another, as you do," Abigail said.

Colin's hand found hers under the table. Even he did not know the extent to which she hated her father and everything he had done to her. Glancing at him she smiled and renewed her resolve to enjoy this time with him. His slight touch was enough to make her heart beat faster. Never had she been handled so gently, and by one whom she suspected could well be a fine pugilist. Strength and tenderness were odd bedfellows, indeed.

Last evening had been aggravating for Abigail as she had been kept away from Colin while Eliza had introduced her to the other guests. His title came with certain responsibilities, his own status as guest notwithstanding. Abigail had hoped today would be different, yet this invitation for tea did not bode well.

Eliza's mother and sisters begged off joining the excursion as they were quite worn out after their journey and the party the previous evening. They would spend the afternoon resting. Abigail was grateful that there would not be such a large audience for whatever was about to unfold. She felt as if she stood at the precipice of something unknown—as if something dark and formidable waited below for her.

All too soon Abigail found herself in the Morgan portrait hall staring at a likeness that anyone could say was of Abigail herself, yet there were subtle differences if one were to be fastidious. Gazing at the canvas, Abigail sought out those variations. The hair that curled perfectly on canvas, the brows that arched femininely over smooth facial features, the smile so like her own. And yet, the eyes spoke of innocent optimism, something that had forever been lacking in Abigail's own life.

She took a step closer to the painting, as if her proximity could alter the fact that this woman was not truly present. Memories of her mother were so faded with time and disuse that this woman may as well have been a stranger, yet there was no denying the tie that bound them together. Those same memories flitted through her mind now as silence filled the gallery. This woman teaching her proper table etiquette, practicing letters and simple spelling, placing herself between Abigail and the anger of an inebriated father.

So caught up was she that she barely registered Colin's hand at her back as he stood sentinel over her. With effort, however, she pulled herself back to the present, thinking how long it had been since she had seen her mother's likeness, as her father had never allowed Abigail to see one, if any had existed at all.

Wiping the tears from her cheeks, she turned to see just how much of a spectacle she had made of herself. However, none of the faces that met her held even an ounce of recrimination or reproach. Instead pity, surprising understanding, and relief filled the room.

"She was your mother, was she not?" Mr. Morgan asked gently.

Not trusting her voice, Abigail could simply nod.

"You do not..." Clearing his raspy throat, Mr. Morgan began again. "You cannot know what finding you means to me. What it will signify for everyone."

"Finding me?" Abigail asked. "Whatever do you mean?"

"This changes everything. Simply everything!" He spoke almost to himself as he turned for the door, excitement radiating through his movements. "Let us retire to the drawing room for tea. There is someone waiting whom I am most anxious for you to meet. And after that, I imagine all will be explained."

The nearly silent journey from the portrait hall to the drawing room seemed to take ages. Had she known she had family apart from her father she would have sought them out long ago. Neither of her parents had ever mentioned them and Abigail had given little thought as to their possible existence. She had never been told the family name so finding them had seemed an impossibility. Knowing now who they were, and *where* they were, could change everything, exactly as Mr. Morgan had said.

For the first time in years Abigail's heart swelled with hope. True hope.

"Quite a surprise, is it not?" Colin mumbled from beside her.

Abigail smiled at him, a smile so filled with joy she thought she might burst. "A most welcome one."

Colin took her hand long enough for a quick squeeze. "It does my heart good to see you so happy."

"My mother died when I was yet a child, years before you and I met," Abigail said, wishing now that she could take the time to speak with him of her mother, yet the drawing room loomed ever closer as they approached.

"I recall you speaking of her from time to time. Your good opinion of her has not lessened with time, I trust?"

"Not a whit," she answered fervently. "I am most anxious to hear more of her, in fact."

"As am I," Colin said softly, causing Abigail to glance out the corner of her eyes at him. How could he seem nearly as anxious to hear of her past as she was herself? Something in his tone made her wonder if there was something else driving his interest in her mother besides curiosity. Before she could ask him, they were led into the drawing room where an aging woman rose from a settee to meet them.

"Heavens," the woman exclaimed with a hand to her mouth, her eyes immediately drawn to Abigail. "You are the very image of her, of my Hannah. What a beauty she was." Tears filled her eyes and Mr. Morgan quickly offered his handkerchief which was snatched with a slight chuckle. "You would think the pain of our loss would have eased after all these years, yet I still feel it acutely. You must pardon this old woman."

Mr. Morgan turned back to his guests, yet continued to address the stranger. "Mama, you have previously met Lord and Lady Bedford as well as Lord Bedford's good friend Lord Haverford." Mr. Morgan, looking quite as pleased as Abigail herself, held his arm out indicating her. "Might I introduce you to Miss Abigail Newell. Miss Newell, Mrs. Isaac Morgan, my mother."

"I am pleased to meet you, Mrs. Morgan," Abigail said with a curtsy.

A grandmama! How many other relatives did she have? Cautiously she waited, wondering how these genteel people would react to her existence.

Mrs. Morgan retook her seat signaling for the others in the room to take their ease. "Come sit with me," she said specifically to Abigail.

Tentatively Abigail sat and attempted to breathe normally. Colin, along with Lord and Lady Bedford receded to the far end of the room, apparently deep in conversation. Abigail was grateful to Colin for giving her a bit of privacy with her newfound family.

"Now tell me," Mrs. Morgan began tensely. "Where is your father?"

Ah, yes. The familiar change in atmosphere that always seemed to accompany mention of that man. Another quick glance at Colin. "I do not know."

A wrinkled yet surprisingly soft hand laid down on her own. "Run off on you, has he? I knew he was a scoundrel from the first."

"Mother," Mr. Morgan warned.

Contrition overtook her countenance. "Of course, my son is right. No matter my feelings for the man, he is still your father. Perhaps it is best we focus on other things. Such as you, my dear. How long have you been staying at Edgemont?"

An easy question, as far as that went. "Less than a week."

A nod. "And how long do you intend to stay?"

A harder question. "It is undecided at present."

"And what do you think of London?"

A surprising question. "London, madam?"

"Yes, London. The Season will be beginning soon, and preparations must be made."

Confusion filled her. "What sort of preparations?"

"Why, preparations for your debut, of course! With neither your mother nor father here, you shall have to make do with this old biddy and her son."

"Mama," Mr. Morgan interjected. "Perhaps we ought to ask Miss Newell—"

Mrs. Morgan interrupted. "'Miss Newell'?" She shook her head emphatically. "No. There will be none of that.

She is Abigail Morgan." Turning back to Abigail, who sat in shocked silence watching the proceedings, she went on. "Now I certainly know that your father's name was not Morgan, but as he has shown his true character I do not wish to remember him each and every time you are addressed, my dear. Your mother was a Morgan, and so shall you be."

Having never had an attachment to any name but her Christian one, Abigail would have previously thought herself open to such a suggestion. The opposite proved true, however. Sitting in this drawing room with these people she scarcely knew, listening to them speak as if she were not present, she felt oddly insulted.

"I believe the name Newell is as useful as any other, Mrs. Morgan, as you have given me no solid reason why I ought to change it now."

"Miss Newell," Mr. Morgan said as he eyed his mother. "My mother and I discussed this yesterday in the wake of our introduction. As there is no doubt in either of our minds as to your being the daughter of my dear departed sister Hannah, we would like to offer you the opportunity to be our guest. My mother and I are soon to return to London, and she would like to sponsor you for this Season."

A moment ticked by before Abigail, disbelieving, asked, "Sponsor me?"

"Yes," Mrs. Morgan said, the light of excitement entering her eyes. "I will provide you with any clothing you stand in need of, jewelry, trinkets, anything within reason. You will stay with us at our townhouse in Mayfair, and Peter will accompany you to balls, soirees, the theatre. What a grand time you shall have."

Abigail felt the room begin to spin. Everything was happening so quickly. They wished her to change her name, to have a proper debut in London, and now to associate with the rest of society in situations she had only ever dreamt of. Needing to ground herself, she asked the only question she felt comfortable with.

"Peter?" Abigail asked.

"As you see, I am getting along in years, my dear," Mrs. Morgan responded, clearly misunderstanding what Abigail was asking. "My stamina is not what it once was. Your uncle will chaperone you quite well."

Abigail glanced at Mr. Morgan, realizing him to be the Peter spoken of. "I see," she said. "And what, precisely, would you expect from me?"

"From you, my dear?" Mrs. Morgan asked. "Well, I suppose the opportunity to get to know you. To hear what sorts of memories you have of my sweet Hannah.

And, of course, you would need to behave yourself as any other young lady of gentility is expected."

Silence reigned once more as the Morgans awaited her answer.

Abigail focused on her breathing, unsure how she could possibly decide such a thing so quickly.

"I believe I need some air. Do you mind?" she asked. She simply needed a few moments to consider what making such a change would mean for her.

"Of course, my dear," Mrs. Morgan said.

Abigail rose and made her way to a window. The sun was hiding behind a cloud, though no rain had fallen. It was the perfect sort of day, neither too hot nor so chilly one would prefer to remain indoors. Yet Abigail found herself wishing for the sun to guide her.

If she were to do this, it could possibly settle her out of her father's reach. Looking from one to the other, Abigail wondered if they would be able to protect her should he come round. She did not know these people, or truly their position in society, yet Mr. Morgan appeared to be a gentleman which was a definitive step higher on the social ladder than her father. The reputation of the Morgans must be such to allow for such consideration from one as prestigious as the marquess and his wife, as Abigail knew they had visited here previously.

Her eyes strayed to Colin once more. Accepting this offer would give her an opportunity to continue socializing with him, under a separate roof, which might keep him more protected as well from the wrath of her father.

Turning back to the window, the cloud moved and the sun shone forth in all its glory. Abigail's heart lifted as she took it to be a sign that she was making the correct decision. Returning to the Morgans, she retook her seat and faced them as they both awaited her response.

"I would be honored to accept your request."

Chapter 11

Colin fingered the parchment in his pocket as he listened to the chatter that evening, knowing that it would show signs of wear as he had been worrying it since receiving it early this morning. He had previously sent Morley off on a mission to Colin's home parish in Somerset. The man was to apply for a common marriage license on Colin's behalf, returning victorious only this morning. Colin could not have known that Peter Morgan would turn Abigail's world upside down this afternoon. And now, Colin could not bring himself to upend Abigail more by adding the weight of another decision to her shapely shoulders.

After dinner, it quickly became apparent that the excitement of the Morgan's revelation continued to feed the women's imaginations. Lady Clara, Eliza's sister, who would also be attending the Marriage Mart, was particularly enthusiastic with the prospect of Abigail being in London for the Season. Lady Gravestone had retired early, leaving the younger set to themselves.

"Blue would look lovely on you, Miss Newell," Clara said, looking up from the book in her hands. "Mama has insisted most of my dresses be some shade of pink."

Eliza smiled. "Mama simply wishes to keep you as her innocent little girl. It is unfortunate that she cannot see how that color drains your complexion. Perhaps rouge will one day be in fashion once more."

"I shudder to think it," Clara said dramatically, before returning her attention to her book. She never seemed to be far away from any sort of reading material, causing Colin to smile.

Abigail watched them with a slight grin. It soothed Colin's heart to see her surrounded by kind ladies near her age. It was a circumstance he had never seen her a part of before.

"You are all three like old hens, making plans and designing wardrobes," he intoned with mock sincerity, attempting to break into their conversation.

"Nevermind him," Eliza said with an arched brow. "He is simply nervous thinking of all the suitors Abigail is certain to attract."

Scowling, he left to join Timothy at the other end of the room. Thoughts of other eligible men entering Abigail's life twisted his gut, making him silent and sulky company. Finally able to take no more of it, he excused himself for the night.

Upon entering his bedchamber, he was surprised to find a note that had been slid under the door in his absence. Curiosity filled him as he bent to retrieve the folded parchment. With Abigail found, he had given little thought to the pursuit of Christopher Wallace, yet he had not recalled his men, nor sent them home. Perhaps one of them had found some clue as to Wallace's whereabouts. Abigail's safety was not yet fully ensured, and Colin would be satisfied with nothing less than her absolute security.

Unfolding the parchment, he read the short message.

My Lord,

Meet me at the before agreed upon location one hour past midnight.

-------D. Kenton

The information Duncan had to share must be rather sensitive, else he would have simply included it in this missive instead of requesting a meeting. Excitement filled him, as he itched to leave this second.

Colin extinguished his candle and looked out the window. In the light of day, the prospect from this room afforded one a wonderful view of the stables. At night however, all that could be seen was an outline of a building slightly darker than the surrounding area. There were no candles burning, signaling the servants would all be sleeping. Knowing that Timothy often enjoyed early morning rides, his servants must be used to retiring early so as to rise in time to see him off.

Perfect.

Slowly opening his door, he quietly made his way outside. He would need to ready his own horse, quietly, not wishing to alert anyone, as his movements required secrecy.

Twenty stress-filled minutes later the night breeze tousled Colin's hair as he rode through the countryside. He hoped he was not taking too long getting to his destination. Being silent in the stables had proven to require a slowness of movement that had tried his patience. It would not do to have Duncan give up and leave before Colin's arrival.

He could scarcely believe Abigail's recent good fortune. The seeming randomness of Colin finding her at Edgemont paled in comparison with this latest development. She now had a legitimate and respectable family, not simply a disreputable father. Means beyond any she had ever known. Opportunities she had never dreamed of. He knew he could offer her more, as a member of the nobility, yet he could not have been more pleased for her.

For himself, however, he was less pleased. As Eliza had so succinctly pointed out mere hours ago, Abigail was now in a position to be courted by any number of useless gentlemen, those who would simply see her outward beauty and care for nothing more. Granted, her financial situation was nowhere near certain. The Morgans were good people, but their wealth was not exactly considerable, and Abigail had mentioned nothing of being offered a dowry along with her sponsored Season. Perhaps he need not worry so much, as most young men seeking suitable wives required such settlements. Colin was blessed indeed not to be in such need, nor did he have living parents pushing him towards making any sort of financial alliances. There was the matter of his sister's opinion to consider, although, if Colin was being honest, her approval was of little importance. He could already predict that she would not be pleased with his choice.

Colin pulled back on the reins, slowing his horse to a walk as he approached the currently abandoned hunting hut at the edge of Timothy's property. Dismounting, he caught his foot on an unseen rock, causing him to fight for balance, but thankfully not causing any lasting damage.

Laughter drew his eyes to the open doorway, where his Bow Street contact stood leaning against the door frame, nearly invisible given the shadow he occupied.

"Forget how to walk, didja?" he asked, evidently not concerned with being overheard. The man's accent was difficult to identify as it seemed to be a conglomerate of multiple dialects.

"Proof that one can never be too careful," Colin replied ruefully as he approached and clapped the man on the shoulder. "It is good to see you, Duncan. Now, do you have any new information for me? Our time here is running short."

"Would I've sent fer ya just to give ya nothin?" Duncan scoffed. "Wallace is still in the wind, but I thought ya oughta know about this." He took a folded parchment from an inside pocket of his coat and held it out for Colin.

Taking the note, Colin quickly scanned its contents by the scant light of the moon, before sliding it into his own pocket. "I assume you have verified this information?"

Duncan's face screwed up in offense. "'Course I did! I been doing this a long time, *Lord Haverford.* I knows my business."

"All right, all right," he said. Colin respected this man, although he could be a might touchy at times. Duncan had been the sole provider of any information Colin had gleaned over the previous few years. It was a matter of damaged pride to Duncan that he had been unable to fully locate Wallace up till now. Duncan's wish to apprehend the criminal matched Colin's own determination over the years to find Abigail. "I meant no harm. I must get back. Lord Bedford needs to be apprised of this situation immediately."

Duncan gave a curt nod, turning to reenter the cottage.

"Gather your men, Duncan," Colin said, halting the other man in his tracks. "We head back to London on the morrow."

Without another word, Duncan was gone, disappearing from sight.

Colin turned back to his horse and mounted quickly. There was work to be done, and the sooner he returned to Edgemont, the better. Timothy needed to know about Wallace's spy that had infiltrated his household.

Approaching the house, Colin felt an inexplicable pull to go to the hidden meadow. Realizing that once he returned to his room preparations for his departure for London would need to be made, he turned his horse south. Venturing to the meadow now would be his final opportunity before leaving the county. Likely Timothy would yet be abed and news of the spy would have to wait.

Entering the meadow, Colin dismounted and walked to the area he had met Abigail previously. Memories swirled through his thoughts as he marveled once more at the surprise of finding her here. That day not so long ago, in the midst of these trees, she had woven her tale of burying a secret. Searching for the exact place where he had come upon her, he was surprised to find the soil disturbed, as if someone had been digging. Why would anyone dig in the precise place he had found Abigail? He recalled the dirt on her fingers that day, the recollection of thinking she was lying to him. What had she buried?

"I knew you would return here," Abigail said from behind him. "You never could conquer your curiosity."

"Perhaps I simply have a wish that needed burying," he said, with a sly wink, somehow unsurprised by her presence.

"Colin?" she asked, taking a tentative step closer.

"Yes?" All thoughts of her previous activities vanished. Abigail filled his vision, growing ever more vital to his further survival. She wore a hooded cloak which only partially hid her cascading tresses, tangled and awry from sleep. How had he lived without her for so many years? She was everything to him. Her eyes held his for a moment, mirroring the emotion he felt. She fluttered her lids, took a step back, and the moment was lost. What had she been about to ask?

"It is good that I found you here," she said. "I feared I would not see you before I left."

Colin reached for her arm. "Do you think I would allow you to disappear once more without saying goodbye?"

Those almond shaped grey eyes gazed into his once more, and he saw the regret in them—the pain. He made a mental note not to mention the past further, as he did not wish to upset her.

Abigail pulled her arm out of his grasp, turning her back to him. "You know that was not my choice."

Colin once more fingered the marriage license he kept in his pocket. Once they married, there would be no more goodbyes, yet something stayed him. He did not wish to begin their lives together on the heels of such memories as their prior separation.

"Is this what you want?" he asked instead. "A proper Season in London?"

She turned back to him, the ghost of a smile on her lips. "Is it not what every young girl wants? To attend balls, and the theatre, and find a husband! Mrs. Morgan says I will have no trouble finding myself a gentleman, regardless of my parents' history. They were properly wed, after all. The truth that my mother's family disapproved does not entirely ruin their reputations."

That was what she wanted? Was the man standing before her now not enough? How could Colin ask her now, when he was not certain she still wanted him?

Releasing the parchment in his pocket, he chose to wait. Having waited these past years to find her, he could wait until she experienced all that London had to offer, and then he would know if he was enough.

Her smile broke through his melancholy. "Since you came to Edgemont, memories have been flashing through my mind." She laughed. "One would think my childhood a happy one, as they are all centered around you. One day, I hope to look back on this Season with similar fondness."

Unable to prevent himself, he took her hand in his own, his longing for her making it difficult to speak. "Will you save me a dance, Abigail?"

Stretching up on her toes, she laid a tender kiss on his cheek, then whispered in his ear, "They will all be yours."

Before he could respond, she turned and ran back in the direction of the house.

Chapter 12

London seemed quite a different city than the loud, filthy slum that Abigail remembered from her previous times spent here, proving that one's station could change everything. Where before she had come as the daughter of a criminal seeking to evade attention, now she was expected to draw attention everywhere she went. She had gone from the cramped, dingy rooms of the local travelers' inns to residing in one of the more modest townhomes in Mayfair.

It had been some weeks since the Morgans had brought her to Town, and Abigail had heard nothing from her father. The familiar sensation of feeling watched at all hours of the day was beginning to ease. She wondered if she could truly have escaped his clutches so easily.

Her days had been filled thus far with visits to the modiste and milliners, shoemakers and jewelers, as well as the many shops in between that sold various accessories. Abigail had initially been appalled by the amount of purchases her grandmother made on her behalf, thinking that Uncle Peter would surely send her away in lieu of paying these bills. Fortunately, Uncle Peter himself had been quick to silence her objections, informing her the money that had been set aside years ago for her mother's dowry was being used to outfit her for the Season. And one could not be presented underdressed.

Uncle Peter had also informed her that whatever funds were left over would become her own dowry. It would not be much, for which he apologized profusely. But he insisted that between what he offered and Abigail's natural charms, she should have no trouble securing a husband.

As overwhelming as this new life had been, Abigail was grateful the Season was not quite fully underway and there had been a surprising, yet pleasant, lack of nightly entertainments. Her grandmother seemed to prefer the quiet life and was determined to enjoy the silence, at least until all of the clothing purchases were received. The downside to staying in was that Abigail had yet to see Colin since her arrival. She told herself that he was busy. As a viscount he would have many responsibilities to see to with the upcoming session of the House of Lords. She could hardly expect him to spend all his time visiting her. But was it too much to expect a single visit?

The many purchases had been steadily trickling in since the beginning of the week, further causing Abigail to blanch with how much had been spent on her. The final delivery arrived just this afternoon. Even now Abigail found herself in all new clothing, including a lovely, albeit simple, gold necklace with a small ruby pendant that she currently rubbed between her fingers. As her new maid Sarah helped her prepare for the evening in silence, Abigail realized she missed the rambling chatter Molly always provided.

A slow rumbling laugh sounded at the doorway to the sitting room where Abigail had been whiling away the time until Uncle Peter descended to escort her to the ballet. Turning, she was surprised to find Colin standing there instead.

"You appear quite scared to death," Colin said as his laughter ceased. "You realize it is simply a night out, not a deportation." He winked.

"You find this humorous?" she asked. "I have never enjoyed a simple night out, as you put it." She walked toward him slowly. "Colin, what if something goes wrong? I have only ever played at being a refined young lady. I was never sent to finishing school, nor learned from any governesses. Even with you here now, I am unsure precisely how to behave."

Colin reached for her hands, pulling her closer. "You will be amazing, Abigail. Truly, you have nothing to fear."

His lack of understanding aggravated her and she pulled her hands away. "What are you doing here?"

"I have come to escort you to the ballet," he said with a flourishing bow.

She could not hide her aggravation with him. He had always drawn out her true feelings. "Why now? We have been in Town for a fortnight."

"Abigail, I would have come sooner if I had been able. You must know that."

Preferring her ire to the fear she had been dwelling in all afternoon, Abigail did not wish to forgive him quite yet.

"And what is it that keeps a lofty viscount so occupied that he cannot spare an afternoon for a friend?" she asked waspishly, hating the words even as they left her lips.

Colin's brow furrowed, clearly unsure how to respond.

Abigail sighed. "Forgive me. I am not myself this evening."

"Is something amiss with the Morgans?" he asked softly. "Have they been unkind to you?"

Abigail smiled, pleased to see his concern, her irritation melting away. "They have been simply wonderful, Colin. They are everything I could have hoped for in a family. Grandmama has nearly exhausted herself taking me from shop to shop buying me all the accoutrements of a genteel lady. And Uncle Peter has been all that a father ought to be."

She hoped Colin would not hear the wistfulness in her voice. She did not wish to be thought ungrateful for what she had, yet could not help longing for more.

"Ah, Lord Haverford," Uncle Peter said as he entered the drawing room. "I am pleased you could join us this evening."

"I am grateful for the invitation. After these past weeks of preparing for the coming session of Lords, I am in desperate need of diversion."

Abigail ought to have known it was something important that had kept Colin away, and not that he wished to distance himself from her. *Foolish girl,* she told herself.

Uncle Peter's eyes turned to Abigail as he kissed her cheek. "You look lovely, my dear."

"Thank you. It is still a bit of a shock to think of all the beautiful things you have given me. I can scarcely believe they are all mine." She indicated her gown which was a lovely soft satin evening dress, light pink in color with tiny flowers embroidered throughout. She had been guided away from choosing too many white fabrics as she was not precisely a debutante, yet told not to stray toward anything too bold.

"You deserve every bit of it," Colin said fervently.

Once they reached the theater, the evening progressed in a whirlwind of introductions as Uncle Peter and Colin seemed to be acquainted with the entire city. Abigail was completely overwhelmed. How was one to be expected to remember them all?

Finding Lord and Lady Bedford amidst the throng was a wonderful reprieve for Abigail, proving that she did in fact know someone. Lady Gravestone and Lady Clara accompanied them. Abigail imagined that she would see Lady Clara often over the next few months, as they would both be paraded before eligible gentlemen. Abigail wondered if a close acquaintance with such a lady would hinder her own chances at finding a suitor. Surely Abigail could not possibly claim as many prestigious invitations as the daughter of an earl. Nevertheless, she would enjoy those events in which they did find themselves together.

Abigail's eyes settled on Colin. Over the past few weeks, she had often considered that if she were truly safe from her father's reach, she might actually be allowed a courtship with him. She had shied away from such thoughts for fear of what her father would do to Colin if he knew of her fondness for him.

Now with Colin here, she found herself once again quite shy as she gazed at him. He spoke to everyone as if he had known them all his life which, she supposed, could be true of some of them. Not knowing the typical way one made acquaintances, she could hardly fault him. It was more a curiosity for her than an irritation. Perhaps watching him would help her master the art of conversing with such well-bred individuals.

Who was she fooling? She simply enjoyed watching him. The strong jaw that softened when he laughed. The eyes that carried his smile and yet could gaze at her as a man dying of thirst staring up at the rain. Those lips that had been both tender and demanding…

A sharp pinch to her elbow drew her out of her thoughts. Lady Clara stood beside her, appearing justified of her recent attack upon Abigail's person. Abigail gaped at her, too aghast at being accosted to make the slightest utterance.

"I believe Miss Morgan and I must visit the retiring room," Lady Clara finally said to the rest of the party. "If you will excuse us."

Lady Gravestone nodded her head in approval and Clara proceeded to lead Abigail through the crowd and into a nearly deserted retiring room. Once the door closed behind them, Lady Clara began to laugh.

"I have scarcely seen anyone so enraptured as you, my dear, appear to be with our dear Lord Haverford," she said once she had regained control of herself. "I do apologize for pinching you, but I thought it better to save you from the spectacle you would have caused had anyone else noticed."

Abigail's face flamed. How could she have been so foolish as to show her interest so openly?

"I suppose it is rather obvious," she admitted, sinking into a settee.

"Oh, Miss Morgan," Lady Clara chuckled as she sat beside her. "You wear your emotions on your face for all to see. It is rather refreshing, if I might be so bold. Not many people in society are so honest; most prefer to keep you guessing what they are thinking. Every utterance has multiple meanings. These women are adept in the art of sounding pretty while they are insulting you."

It was a testament to how little Lady Clara knew her that she would consider Abigail to be honest. Yet, in a way, the lady was correct. Was Abigail losing her ability to hide her true emotions? Frustration with herself welled up within her and she focused on pushing the sensation away once more. Taking a deep breath, she calmed her racing heart. She must regain her focus before she was entirely upended. Looking at Lady Clara once more, she realized she could truly use a friend.

"What can I do?" she asked. Not wishing to completely open herself up to a woman who was still largely a stranger to her, she added, "I was not brought up for this life. I lack the training." It was best to keep this conversation mostly superficial.

Lady Clara patted Abigail's knee affectionately. "You bide with me. This is not my first Season, and I would be pleased to help you learn to navigate society."

Abigail could not help being suspicious. In her experience one did not offer assistance without requiring something in return. "Why would you do that for me? You hardly know me."

Clara looked pensive. "To be truthful, I have been rather lonely since my sister married. Before she met the marquess, we were nearly inseparable. I would prefer not to go about this business of finding a husband on my own."

"Lady Clara—"

"Clara, please."

"That does sound appealing. However, I see one large flaw with your proposition. Regardless of how I address you, you are the daughter of a countess and the sister-in-law of a marquess. There is no nobility within my family lines. That is, none that I am aware of. You will certainly receive vastly different invitations than I. In truth, my friendship with your sister, as well as Lord Haverford, are truly the best recommendations I have, and they can only be called upon so many times before all of society will know I have little to recommend myself."

Clara thought for a moment, her excitement slipping, but not becoming fully extinguished. "You clearly do not understand the aristocracy. Connections can be a massive source of power, and having the ear of a marchioness is nothing to scoff at." Her eyes narrowed slyly. "I believe Eliza will be more than capable of securing you invitations to whichever entertainments we choose. Do not worry, Miss Morgan…"

"Abigail."

Clara smiled fully. "Do not worry, Abigail. You leave the matter of invitations to me."

Abigail had seen enough plots being formed to know that one was working its way through Clara's mind. Yet every plot came with a price. Would Abigail be willing to pay the price of Clara's? With such a short acquaintance, it was anyone's guess. Despite herself, Abigail found herself wishing to go along with the young woman.

"Let us be clear," she found herself saying. "You will keep me from causing embarrassment to myself or my relatives? And in return you simply wish for me to accompany you to every society event you attend?"

"Quite right," Clara said with hope in her eyes.

"Very well. A friend is such a rare find that I would be foolish to turn down your offer."

Clara clasped her hands together in excitement. "What an enjoyable Season this will be, Abigail. You have truly relieved a weight off my mind."

Smiling in return, Abigail stood. "We ought to get back. The ballet is sure to be beginning."

"Of course."

Abigail left the retiring room much more at ease than she had entered it. Perhaps Clara was correct, and this Season could truly be enjoyable. Possibilities began running through her mind and her smile grew.

They made their way through the crowd of people moving to their own boxes and seats. She registered one person just before fear coursed through her entire being. Her blood drained from her face and she began to feel light-headed. The room began to spin, and the faces around her seemed to somehow multiply, yet one face stood in stark contrast with all the rest. Darkness encompassed her and she fell to the ground, unconscious.

Her father.

Chapter 13

Colin had to admit, watching Abigail walk away was not an altogether negative prospect. His appreciative eyes remained on her as Lady Clara maneuvered her way through the throng.

"And how is your sister?" Mrs. Willowby asked. She waved her fan quite deliberately before her, the heat of the crush turning the tips of her nose and ears pink. It only enhanced Colin's fondness for the older woman who seemed to genuinely care about his welfare.

Colin pitied the woman. A kindly soul, and one he had much respect for. She had married midway through her first Season many years ago, and widowed after the war with the Colonies. He had left her alone to raise their only child, a son rarely seen in society, though Colin was ignorant of the cause. Colin had wondered often at her not marrying once more. However curious he was, that was not a topic easily spoken of within the *ton*—at least not within earshot of the person involved.

"I have not seen her for some time, I am afraid. She is off to the continent at present. I believe she intends to return by Michaelmas."

"Ah," the woman smiled knowingly, aware as she was of Colin's feelings toward Charlotte. "You will send her my regards?"

"Of course, my lady."

They parted, and Colin glanced once more in the direction Abigail and Lady Clara had gone. They ought to have returned by now.

"It is time for us to find our seats," Lady Gravestone said, as he approached. "Where have those girls taken themselves off to?"

Colin looked over her shoulder and was relieved to find Abigail and Lady Clara exiting the retiring room at last. Relief gave way to great fear clutching at his chest as he watched Abigail's color drain away and she slumped first against Lady Clara, then dropped unceremoniously to the ground.

Colin burst toward her, unheeding of the exclamations that followed him. Kneeling at her side, he raised her head in his hands.

"Abigail?"

No response.

Lowering his head to hers, he listened for signs of life. Hearing none, he looked up as Mr. Morgan knelt across from him, the man's expression one of businesslike calm. Placing a finger beneath her nose, he looked up with assurance in his eyes.

"She is breathing."

"Thank God!" Colin croaked.

Timothy could be heard behind Colin. "Clara, what happened?"

"I-I don't know. She was fine. We were coming back to find you and suddenly down she went."

"She said nothing before? Gave you no indication she was ill?"

"No. Nothing." Lady Clara looked around her. "Would she have seen someone who could have frightened her?"

Colin heard the commotion around them, felt the suffocating crush of bodies as onlookers whispered back and forth.

"We cannot leave her here," Mr. Morgan said. "I will call for my carriage. We will get her home and send for the doctor."

"Of course." Colin nodded, and both men jumped to action.

Sliding his arms under Abigail's limp form, he rose, carrying her through the crowd and out into the chill night air. With the breeze she began to stir, yet she did not awaken. Soft moans came from her throat. Her head rose from its slumped position to snuggle into Colin's chest. He had longed for such closeness, but not for this reason.

As he spoke a steady stream of soothing words, he wished he could comfort himself. He blamed himself for not being beside her. He told himself he could not have prevented her from seeing to her own needs, nor did he wish to be her jailer. Yet how could he protect her if she was not with him every moment?

After placing her within her uncle's carriage, he too embarked. One look at Mr. Morgan silenced the other man's objections and they were quickly off to the Morgan's townhouse. Upon arriving, Abigail was laid out on a divan in the nearest drawing room.

Mr. Morgan barked orders to the butler to fetch the doctor, while a maid was sent to prepare a pot of strong tea. Colin pulled a high-backed chair near the divan and settled himself. Taking up one of Abigail's hands, he caressed it within his own.

Some of her color began to return to her face, and her fingers twitched at his touch. Her eyelids fluttered, and then they flew open. Flailing her arms she yelled out, sitting upright and flying away from him.

"Where is he?" she screamed. "Where is he?"

"Abigail!" Colin called back to her, trying to grasp her hand once more. "Abigail, calm yourself!"

Her eyes trained on his, and for a moment he saw a wild, haunted look cross her face. What he would give to never see such a look again. And then she was in his arms, great sobs shaking her slight frame.

"Colin, Colin!" she cried.

"I am here, darling," he soothed.

Colin looked helplessly at Mr. Morgan who watched his niece's histrionics with a flabbergasted expression. There would be little assistance from that quarter. A few more moments passed, her cries becoming more constant, with him rubbing soothing circles on her back.

A throat cleared from the doorway and Colin turned to see who was there. The doctor had arrived carrying his case of supplies. Colin slowly eased Abigail away, helping her to sit on the divan once more. The wildness had left her eyes, but they remained red-rimmed and wet with tears.

"I would ask you to leave us while I examine the patient," the doctor said curtly. Mr. Morgan escorted

Colin into the corridor, shutting the door behind them to allow for privacy with Abigail's examination.

"I presume," Mr. Morgan began, "you know as little of this outburst as I?"

Colin's cravat suddenly felt tight as guilt washed over him. Perhaps he ought to have been more forthcoming with this man about Abigail's history. Yet how much of it was Colin's story to tell? If Abigail had wished for her uncle to know about her upbringing, would she not have broached the subject herself?

"I know she has bad dreams," he allowed, "on occasion."

The older man's scowl spoke to his dissatisfaction.

Colin rubbed a hand over his forehead. "Her father was less than genteel, often drunk, a thief...and quite abusive."

"Ah," Mr. Morgan intoned with understanding. "I knew very little of Christopher Egerton as I was away at university when he came to town. My father never approved of the man, but I never had a good understanding as to why. When Hannah eloped with him, my parents refused to speak more on the subject."

Christopher Egerton?

Colin took a moment to run the name through his head a few times, intent on remembering it so as to pass it along to Duncan.

"You will not hear more of it from Abigail," he finally added.

"I thought not. She measures her words carefully and has refused to speak of her life before we met."

"I am not surprised. I have known her since we were young, and she rarely speaks of those things with me, either. I hope to one day make her see that she can trust me."

Mr. Morgan eyed him carefully. "One day, she will see that."

The drawing room door opened and the doctor emerged.

Colin rushed to question him. "How is she?"

The man raised a soothing hand. "She will recover. It appears to be nothing more than a weak constitution. Miss Morgan assures me that her episode this evening is nothing unheard of for her, and she often recovers fully after a restful night's sleep. I have left her doing just that, and I must insist upon her not being interrupted further this evening."

"Of course, Doctor." Mr. Morgan showed the man to the door, which was just a few feet from where they all had stood. "Thank you for your prompt assistance."

The door closed after the doctor, and Colin, realizing he had no legitimate reason to stay, also took his leave, promising to return early the next morning.

He had not made it far before his feet led him to cross to the other side of the street to stand across from Abigail's townhouse. He simply could not bring himself to leave her. Not wishing to be caught out by the watchman near the end of the row, however, he cowered behind bushes like a common pickpocket.

The doctor's diagnosis ought to have calmed Colin's fears. Try as he might, something niggled at the back of his mind. Abigail had never been one with a weak constitution. Never had he known her to swoon. Yet she led the doctor to believe she did. She had been well when they arrived at the theater, and then had fainted not twenty minutes later. What could have happened during that time to make her so weak?

The sound of raucous laughter and the rumbling of wheels grew louder as a carriage drew past him, stopping a few doors away. A group of young men alit, falling against one another as they stumbled up the stairs entering what must be a bachelor's residence. Colin shook his head at the young men scarcely out of leading strings. Rarely had he fallen so into his cups as to make such a fool of himself. The night of Abigail's disappearance had been the first exception. He had learned that night he was not a merry drunkard. No, he veered more toward the morose. And that discouragement had lasted long after the spirits had disappeared.

Think, man!

Lady Clara was under the impression that Abigail saw someone as she exited the retiring room which gave her a fright. Could that be it? Who could elicit such fear in Abigail as to cause such a reaction?

Christopher!

Cursing the propriety that insisted he not be with her now, Colin moved to go home where he would send for Duncan. If Christopher Wallace was indeed in London, Abigail would not be safe.

Before he had gone more than a few feet, he saw the door to the Morgan's townhouse open. Ducking behind a nearby tree, he watched as a hooded figure slipped out. The shadow turned at the sidewalk and began lightly running toward the end of the street.

"What the devil?" Colin muttered as he sprang into action, chasing the person as silently as possible. They would likely run faster once alerted to Colin's pursuit.

The figure turned west, heading closer to Colin's own street. As Colin was familiar with this area it was easy to guess the destination—Hyde Park. Curiosity had forever been Colin's downfall, and he could not deny the pull of it now. This person was too slight to be a man, yet too large to be a child. As the widow Morgan could have no cause to be out in the midst of the night, Colin could assume this was either Abigail or a maid out on some nefarious business. The former required his protection, and the latter would likely link back with Abigail in some way. Regardless, Colin pressed on.

Cursing, Colin ducked around the corner of a stone wall as the woman turned, glancing behind her. Peering around the corner, Colin saw that it was indeed Abigail. Did she instinctively know she was being followed, or had he been heard? Being stealthy had never been a talent of his.

He wished to approach her, shake some sense into her, and return her to her uncle. How could he protect her when she took such careless risks? A lone woman on the streets of London was never a safe venture, and it was made worse under the cover of darkness where any sort of depraved lunatic might accost her.

Peeking around the wall once more, Colin cursed once more to find her much farther down the street than he would have guessed. He was able to gain on her once more just as she entered the park.

Right before Colin entered, he saw another figure slipping through the shadows of the trees. His heartbeat quickened. He had not ventured out this night prepared for a street brawl. Rarely did one attend the ballet equipped for protection. If he could, it would be best to avoid any open conflict, however he would protect Abigail at all costs. If this new individual chose to approach her, then Colin would act.

Abigail left the paved paths, cutting across the open grassy expanse illuminated dimly by the sliver of moon overhead. Before entering a small copse of trees on the banks of the Serpentine, she halted, turning to look in all directions. Colin crouched behind a nearby hedge. Watching in fascination, he saw the man following Abigail drop quickly to the ground to also avoid detection.

Turning his focus back to Abigail, he watched her bend down for a moment, then rise once more and begin walking back in his same direction. Unable to prevent her progress, she would soon encounter her pursuer. Rising to his full height, he sprinted toward the two. He must have made some sound, for Abigail's head swung in his direction briefly before she turned and ran in an entirely new direction.

Indecision gripped him. Ought he to overtake Abigail? See her home safely? Or take out his frustrations on her would-be assailant? The choice was made for him as the other man rose up, charging at Colin. Diving head first, Colin rolled as the man reached for him. Tumbling, he caught his feet once more, taking a fighting stance, ready to meet this attacker. The aggressor, however, chose to use that brief moment to get away, running back in the direction they all had come from.

Free from that danger, Colin looked around for Abigail, but she was gone. Vanished in the night as if she had never been there. He bent over, hands on his knees, and took measured breaths in an attempt to regain his composure. Rising, he cursed his lack of foresight. Duncan ought to have been guarding the Morgan's townhouse. Colin's complacency had led to this situation.

Realizing the night need not be a complete waste, Colin walked purposefully to the copse of trees Abigail had stopped near. As he searched the nearby ground, he located a folded parchment at the base of a tree, held in place by a rock hardly the size of a small egg. Stooping, he picked up the rock, the paper fluttering from underneath it. Colin quickly grasped the note to prevent the wind taking it.

The hair on the back of Colin's neck stood on end as he feared the worst. Hands shaking, he unfolded the paper, hoping not to find what he knew would be within. By the light of the moon he could barely discern to whom it was addressed.

Father,

Heart sinking, he crumpled the note in his hand. There was no need to read the signature. She had told him there was no contact, that she did not know Christopher's whereabouts. His mind flashed to the times he had suspected—no, known—that she was lying to him. He had dismissed his doubts, unable to face the harsh reality. Abigail was not the woman he remembered from his past. She had deliberately deceived him. And he had willingly played the fool.

His resolve stiffened, along with his backbone. He quickly read the missive, committing it to memory. Then he refolded the paper and placed it once more under the stone, exactly as he had found it.

Returning home, Colin insisted his butler accompany him to his study. By the light of his man's candle, Colin pulled the necessary writing implements from his desk, dashing off a note to Duncan arranging a meeting for the following morning. He felt only a moment's regret over keeping his trusted servant up at such an hour.

"See this gets to Duncan immediately," he said by way of direction. All his trusted men knew Duncan and how he could be contacted.

Left alone, Colin sank into his desk chair. Pulling another paper from his pocket, he stared down at the marriage license. How could he have been naive enough to believe he could simply propose to Abigail and all would be well? How could he make such a commitment if Abigail would not be honest with him? As a viscount, he had responsibilities; he was no laborer free to marry any woman of his choosing. Abigail had little enough to recommend herself, aside from Colin's seemingly unending love for her. She possessed no wealth, no station, had developed no accomplishments that any refined young lady ought to have done. Yet Colin simply could not let her go.

Knowing the truth of Abigail's betrayal, he loved her still. His trust in her may have been broken, but his love? It would appear as if his was everlasting. And the devil take him, but he would save her yet, even if that meant protecting her from herself.

Chapter 14

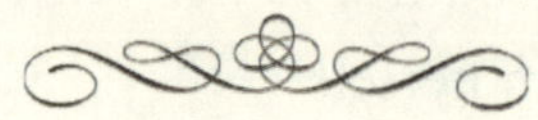

"Do you know," Clara leaned in to say, "I have always loved a ball. One can fully fade into the background and yet enjoy the setting."

However unnerving it was to participate with the mass of people within this current crush of the Baron Winthrop's ballroom, Abigail would concede the setting was beautiful. It was not the countless strangers she currently faced which had her legs shaking and her hands balled into fists. Biting her lower lip, she took her time peering from face to face, hoping not to see her father once more.

Three days had passed, with this being her first time out of the house since her clandestine adventure the night she had seen her father at the ballet. Now Abigail found herself searching for him everywhere. They had not spoken, or even met since, although she had managed to send him a message. Memories of that night still sent a shiver down her spine. The fear that had dogged her steps as she made her way to their secret spot in Hyde Park, and the fright upon being discovered. She had run until she could no longer breathe, and even after locking the front door behind her she did not feel safe. She could only imagine her father's rage at finding her gone from Edgemont and having to hunt her down. By reaching out to him now, she hoped to staunch some of that anger.

"You do not appear to be enjoying yourself, my dear."

Abigail ripped her eyes away from her search and back to those of her companion. Clara's held compassion and concern.

"Forgive me," Abigail said, making a mental effort to relax her muscles. "It is perhaps a bit too soon for me to be venturing out once more. I am yet a bit weak." She had managed to play off her episode the other day as being due to her courses, an ailment which brooked no further discussions, yet drew sympathy from all. "Perhaps we could simply sit for a while?"

"Certainly." Despite Clara's own interest in attracting a husband, she was proving to be a rather altruistic friend.

Clara murmured something to her mother, then grasping Abigail by the arm led her out of the ballroom and down a corridor. Abigail glanced behind, the hair on the back of her neck rising with her dismay at leaving the safety of the crowd. Her father could do little to her in public, aside from ruining what reputation she had as the relation of a gentleman. In private, however, he would not hold back his anger.

The chamber they entered appeared to be the library. From what little Abigail had learned about Clara it made perfect sense that the lady would know the location of such a room.

Clara smiled ruefully. "The baron is quite an avid reader. Last Season, upon discovering my proclivity for it as well, he opened his library to me. I have visited many times and have never failed to find a volume of interest. I have also yet to see another person while within this room. I believe you will have plenty of room to breathe here."

Interest in books? Abigail's own life was so like a gothic novel that she felt no desire to read anything similar. Clara must have noticed her reticence as she led Abigail to a settee facing the door, it's back to the open fireplace. Ample windows flanked the dying fire, with curtains as tall as the room. Was there an unnatural bulge behind that one?

"Here now," Clara said gently, drawing Abigail's attention away from the devils she seemed to find everywhere. "You sit while I fetch some ratafia and something to nibble on."

Abigail clutched at Clara's arm. "Please stay with me," she asked, thinking once more of the curtains and what could be lurking behind them.

Am I going mad?

Clara's eyebrows scrunched. "You are quite pale. Perhaps I ought to find Mr. Morgan and have him see you home."

"No," Abigail sighed as she steadied herself. She did not wish to disturb anyone else's evening. Forcing a smile, she said, "I believe you are right. With a quick rest and a little nourishment I shall be myself once more." This was not the way she had envisioned her very first ball. Where were her dances with all of the eligible young gentlemen? What of her dance she had promised Colin before leaving Shropshire?

Clara stared at her for a moment, then said, "I shall not be gone long," and left.

Abigail hoped Clara was correct, and all she needed was to take a few moments to right herself. Shifting around, Abigail attempted to find a comfortable position. The size of the furniture was such that lying down was quite impossible for anyone over the age of three. She tried turning sideways and lifting her legs up under her, arranging her skirts appropriately so as to avoid embarrassment should anyone else enter. Leaning her head on her hand she propped it up on the back of the settee. This position offered a modicum of comfort, although she longed to be within her own bedchamber at home.

Home.

The thought nearly brought a smile to her face. So quickly had she begun to think of the house she resided in with her uncle and grandmother as being her home. Since her mother's death, she had never considered herself as having one. Such a delicious sensation it was to feel as if one belonged somewhere, with someone.

A rustle near the window drew her attention. Turning, she watched in horror as her father stepped out from behind a curtain.

I was right!

"Would be better for you, Abby, to wipe that grin off your face," he growled.

"P-Papa!" She jumped off the settee, backing away from him.

His beady, bloodshot eyes burned through her, yet somehow turned her blood ice cold. She had seen him angry in the past, but that could not touch the rage she registered on his face now.

"You ought to be ashamed of yourself," he sneered. "Running off like a common trollop!"

"N-no," she stumbled back against an ottoman, barely righting herself before going down. "I l-left you a note, in our place," she lied. "D-did you n-not receive it?"

As fast as she backed away, he was quicker. Catching her by the arm with one hand he raised the other, ready to strike.

Cringing, she prepared for the blow. Before it landed, the door behind her father opened.

"Abigail?"

Her father's arm came down, and he quickly smoothed her sleeves, attempting to hide what he had been prepared to do.

Abigail glanced over his shoulder and was surprised to find Eliza on the threshold. Moving past her father, she tried to keep the quiver out of her voice.

"Yes?"

Eliza's eyes darted from Abigail to her father and back once more, clearly puzzled.

"I spoke with Clara who told me you were feeling ill. I simply came to check on you."

Abigail moved so as to keep her father as hidden behind her as possible. The shame of admitting to this lady that such a man was her father was more than she could bear.

"You are too kind, Eliza," Abigail answered. What must this proper lady think of her now? The obvious explanation was too horrifying to think on. Eliza must leave the room before her father said something that would incriminate her further. "I will return to the ballroom momentarily."

"Now, now," her father said from behind her, drawing the attention of both women. Thankfully, the man had dressed for the occasion, appearing for all as if he belonged. "There is no such rush, my dear." He stepped out from behind Abigail. "What a beautiful piece that is," he said, indicating the ruby necklace Eliza wore. "Only once before have I seen such a necklace."

Abigail noted the greed within his eyes, yet there was something more than that hidden in their depths. Some emotion lurking just below the surface, one that perplexed Abigail. Was it nostalgia? It seemed almost as if her father recognized the jewelry. How could that be? Abigail was certain he had never before met Eliza. Perhaps he had seen her wear it previously, although that would mean that Christopher Wallace had been watching the lady long before Abigail knew her.

"Thank you," Eliza answered with a hand reaching up to caress the ruby. "It belonged to my husband's mother.

I inherited it upon my marriage to the Marquess of Bedford."

Abigail was momentarily speechless. With Eliza having been in mourning for her own father since her marriage to Timothy, she would not have had occasion to wear such jewelry. In such a case, her father would have had to have been acquainted with Timothy's own mother to have seen the necklace before. Was such a thing possible? Could all of their lives have been somehow intertwined long before now?

Her father inched closer to Eliza, who kept her hand protectively over the gem. His eyes focused on the ring she wore on the hand covering the necklace. It was intricate, though much smaller than the gems residing in the necklace or the earbobs Eliza also wore. Why would such a thing so draw his interest?

Apparently realizing that no introduction would be forthcoming from Abigail, Eliza began backing out. "I really ought to be getting back. Lord Bedford will be missing me. I simply wished to see how you were, Abigail. I am gratified to know you are up and recovering. I know Lady Clara was fetching you some refreshment and will be back any moment." If fleeing a room can be done elegantly, Eliza did so. However, she had no way of knowing what sort of a maniac she was leaving behind with Abigail.

Once the door closed, her father whirled back, slapping Abigail across the face with the back of his hand, knocking her back several paces. Before she could recover, he grasped two fistfuls of her hair, yanking her side to side. Hairpins fell unheeded as Abigail suppressed a scream. Her hands flew to cover his as she desperately pulled to free herself. She scratched at his arms, his hands, anything she could find.

Releasing her, he hit her once more, and she fell back, landing on the same settee she had rested on minutes before.

"Stupid girl. I ought to have put you out years ago! All this time, feeding you, clothing you, *teaching* you, and for what?" He took to pacing in front of her. "I gave you everything! And yet you cannot accomplish the one thing I have asked of you. You are as worthless as your mother."

Abigail sat in complete shock. It was not that such outbursts were unusual, rather that he had spoken of her mother. He had not once mentioned her since the day she had died, leaving Abigail alone in her grief. What had prompted him to speak of her now?

"I-I have tried..." Abigail began.

"You have failed!" he yelled. "And what is more, you ran." Leaning down so he was face to face with her, his eyes reflected the fire behind her as if his very soul burned with hatred. He whispered, "You will never be free of me. Wherever you go, whatever you do, I will always find you."

Abigail's spine shivered as the truth of his words penetrated through her fear. She needed to placate him, before he did something she would never recover from.

"The lady trusts me, Father." She nearly choked on the title, for he had never been a true father to her. "I am in her confidence. I can yet succeed!"

"I was fool enough to believe that once," he ground out. "Fool indeed to think there could be any use for you."

Abigail pushed herself up from the settee, attempting to speak to him on his level, not as a victim cowering before master. "Please, Father. A little more time, that is all I need."

"How?" he asked. "You are no longer a guest of theirs."

"There is not time to discuss it now." A fact that aided her as she had no idea how she would actually be able to accomplish such a thing. "Lady Clara will be here momentarily."

Christopher grabbed her by the ear, yanking her around furniture toward the fireplace.

"You have until week's end. If you fail me again," he said, his voice ringing with venom, "I will do to you as with these logs. I hear death by fire is not a pleasant way to die, but I have yet to see it myself. Simply give me an excuse." He pushed her by her ear onto her knees, her face so near the heat of the flames her eyes stung. She heard the rustle of his footsteps as he retreated through the open window he must have come through upon his arrival, leaving her on the floor, tears flowing down her cheeks.

A moment later, she heard the snick of the door opening once more.

"I am afraid I was waylaid at the refreshment table," Clara said from the doorway. "Mother insisted that I speak with Mr. Thompkins. He is a nice enough gentleman, although a bit loquacious…" A slight pause, and Abigail heard rather than saw her put down a drink. Abigail's eyes still stared unseeing into the fire before her.

"Abigail?" Clara asked, her skirt rustling as she moved to look around the room. She came around from the other side of the settee and saw Abigail sitting on the floor. What a sight she must have been!

"Oh!" Clara exclaimed, rushing to kneel with Abigail. "What has happened to you?" Clara's hands tentatively touched Abigail's hair, attempting to smooth away the disarray. Her soft fingers gently touched her sore cheek. Abigail sniffed, and Clara found a handkerchief from a hidden pocket of her gown and began to wipe Abigail's face for her.

"I-I..." Abigail tried between sobs.

"Hush," Clara soothed. "You need not speak of it now if you do not wish it. Come, let us get you presentable."

Sitting sideways on the settee with her back to Clara, the lady did what she could to fix Abigail's hair. The care with which Clara performed her ministrations was remarkable and did much to calm Abigail's frail state of mind.

"It will not be as elegant as it was before." Clara said. "I am no coiffeur, yet it ought not to draw the eyes of those we pass on our way out. Now we will find your uncle and get you home as soon as possible."

With her breathing slowed and her pulse steadied, Abigail allowed Clara to lead her out of the library.

Chapter 15

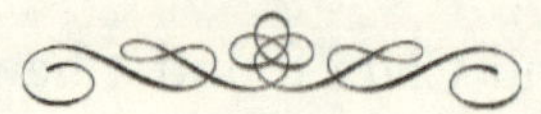

The opening of the curtains in his bedchamber blinded Colin when Morley set about his morning tasks. Rolling away from the sudden light, he moaned his displeasure, which did not prevent the man from continuing to hum in a most ridiculous manner.

Rarely did Colin sleep so late. Having not arrived home until the early hours of morning, combined with his new mixed emotions regarding Abigail, left him no desire to rise. He had spent the majority of the past few days at his club, drowning himself as he attempted to make sense of what was happening around him. He felt listless, unsure how to proceed. He had not felt this upended since his father had passed several years before.

There were no pressing matters that required his attention. No longer did he have his quest to recover Abigail driving him. Even his hunt for Wallace had lost his interest, as he cared little for recovering his family's stolen wealth. His sole purpose in finding that man had been to find his daughter. With that accomplished, Colin found himself rather listless. The recent proof of her lies about being in contact with her father left Colin with little reason to go about his regular routine.

A knock on his door roused him further. Leaning up on his elbows, he ignored the pounding in his head and looked past his bedpost toward the door. With Morley and himself already in the room, Colin could not guess who would be at his door at this time of day. Morley set aside Colin's clothing to answer it. The aggravating man held the door just so as to prevent Colin from seeing the newcomer. Knowing his uncharacteristically cruel thoughts to be proof of his sour disposition, he rose, hoping to find some other way to engage his thoughts.

After speaking briefly with the unseen person on the other side, Morley then turned back, closing the door once more.

"What news, Morley?" Colin muttered, then splashed water on his face, his curiosity overpowering his ennui.

"Visitors, my lord," came the clipped reply as the man set back to his tasks once more.

"Visitors? As in, more than one?" He dried his face and hands, tossing the towel to his valet who caught it up adroitly and hung it near the window to dry.

As a bachelor living on his own, Colin rarely entertained. His sister, Lady Charlotte Haddington, occasionally deigned to stop in, always on her own as her elderly husband had passed shortly after their nuptials. With her prickly disposition, Colin doubted she had any friendships which would extend to a visit with her only remaining relative. Timothy was the only other occasional visitor, although they typically met at the Bedford townhouse or their mutual club.

"As in," Morley mimicked, drawing a deeper scowl from his master, "three."

"Who?"

Morley smiled in evident delight over Colin's ignorance. "Lord and Lady Bedford."

Colin waited, not wishing to rise to the obvious bait, but unable to contain himself. "And?" he prompted.

"And we ought to be getting you dressed."

Moving Colin's arms as one would with an uncooperative child, Morley worked on his task taking away the wrinkled tunic his master wore.

Upon making Colin presentable, Morley handed him a goblet filled with a sort of brown sludge and instructed him to pinch his nose and drink.

"For your head, my lord," he answered the unasked question.

"Are you attempting to kill me, Morley?" Colin asked flatly. "Have we truly come to this?"

The man was enjoying this far too much. Colin had known Morley for a decade or more and never had he been led astray. Colin guzzled it down, gagging on the last bit. As he opened his mouth to hurl any number of curses at the servant, he realized that he was already beginning to feel more himself.

"What on earth have you given me?" he asked instead.

"An occupational secret, my lord." He indicated the door. "Your guests are waiting."

Morley refused to divulge any further information. And since his valet had now finished his ministrations, Colin had no reason not to go down.

Perhaps Abigail would be calling on him. She certainly could, seeing as it would be in the company of a highly respected couple within society. As he had stayed away these past days, he could only imagine what she must be thinking. She had never been one to force her company on others when it was within her power, preferring people to go to her, rather than seek out any attention. It was just as well, as Colin was still uncertain as to his feelings toward her. His ire at finding her still in contact with Wallace had largely dissipated these past few days, yet still lingered in the background.

Barring Abigail, Timothy could have brought any number of people to Colin's home, though not one other name stood out as a likely candidate.

Leaving his valet to his work of setting the room to rights, he headed for the drawing room. Taking the stairs down two at a time, he entered said room moments later to find Lady Clara as the third visitor.

"To what do I owe the honor of this visit, Lady Clara?" he asked with a lavish bow. "Your lovely sister may be obligated to show such attention as she is married to my oldest friend, yet you are bound by no such ties."

Lady Clara smiled, seemingly amused by his antics. "Perhaps I simply wished for some amusement, my lord."

Colin clicked his tongue. "I believe we all do, my lady." He was beginning to like Eliza's sister. She possessed a sense of humor beneath her somewhat quiet exterior, something he could appreciate in a woman.

Timothy shifted away from the window he had been gazing out of. "That is enough. Colin, we must speak to you of Abigail."

Fear clenched Colin's chest, as it often had these past few days. "What has happened?" he demanded.

He took another look at Lady Clara. What Timothy had to say must be of some import for him to bring up such a subject within Lady Clara's presence. Annoyance at another person becoming embroiled in his mess of affairs replaced his fear and he found himself glancing longingly at the sideboard that contained a decanter of sherry. Was nine o'clock in the morning too soon for a drink?

Frustration with his oscillating emotions filled him. As Timothy recounted the happenings of the previous evening at Lord Winthrop's ball, Colin could not release his sense of responsibility. It had been his choice to not attend the event. Just before he was due to leave for the Baron's ball, Duncan had sent a note summoning him. The information the man had shared had seemed, at the time, well worth missing one event. Following his rendezvous, Colin had returned to his club in lieu of arriving late to the ball.

Unable to remain still, he rose and took to pacing, careful to remain out of reach of any of his guests. The last thing he wished for at present was a hand on his arm offering comfort.

"Colin," Timothy said gently, "I know you are upset..."

Turning quickly to face his friend, Colin responded through clenched teeth, "You can have no idea..." He gulped down large amounts of air, not knowing what to do with the enormous emotions running through him.

"I should have been there!" he shouted, slamming his hands down hard on the back of a chair. The resulting sting was less than he deserved.

Timothy moved closer, attempting to soothe him, yet careful to stay out of reach. "It is likely you could have done nothing to prevent what has happened. And in the eyes of the law, Christopher Wallace has every right to do what he pleases with his own daughter. The way things stand, you cannot keep her from him."

"The eyes of the law?" he repeated. He could feel the tentacles of the demented entering his mind, as he indeed felt rather mad. "When the law allows a woman to be battered and bruised, placing all authority into the hands of that abuser, I cease having a care for the law." Colin's fingers curled into balls at his sides, and the room suddenly felt too warm, too close.

"Then I suggest you do something about it," Lady Clara said from across the room, sounding for all the world to be a voice of reason. Colin wondered once more why she was being included in this.

Pushing his question aside, he slipped his hand into his coat pocket where the marriage license yet resided. Slowly pulling it out, he unfolded it and handed it to Timothy.

"What is this?" Timothy asked, his eyes scanned the official document, then widened in surprise. "How long have you had this?"

"Nearly a month," Colin admitted. "I sent Morley to Somerset for it while we were yet at Edgemont. There has scarcely been a moment of peace since, and I have not had occasion to speak with her about it."

An exasperated expulsion of air sounded from Eliza. With a look of clear annoyance, she addressed Lady Clara. "I abhor it when the two of them do this, speaking as if the entire room knew what they were about." She turned to Timothy. "What are the two of you jabbering about?"

Handing the parchment to his wife, Timothy answered, "A marriage license, useless as it stands, as we are past the dates of use. Were he to propose to Abigail now, he would need to procure a new one."

Large smiles appeared on the faces of both women, and Eliza clapped her hands together. "That would solve everything," she said.

"Hardly everything," Lady Clara scoffed, though her smile lingered.

Yes, he was definitely coming to like Eliza's sister. She often had her nose in a book, true. Yet she had a brain hidden behind her fair facade, if one chose to listen when she spoke, which he did now.

"If you simply marry her," Lady Clara continued, "there would be little to prevent her father from continuing to cause her, or yourself, my lord, additional harm. He would be free to pursue her, or blackmail you. There would be no limit to the embarrassment such a relation could cause. We all have enough experience with the *ton* to know that one poorly bred relation can certainly spell ruin for the entire family."

She glanced from person to person, a needless gesture as she commanded the attention of the entire room. "What I have in mind would ensure the man cannot harm you, or Abigail, ever again. It is a long-term solution. One which may be difficult to see to fruition, yet would ensure the most happiness that can come from a situation such as this."

Hearing the lady speak in such a manner, her presence suddenly made perfect sense to Colin, and he was grateful to his friends for bringing her along. Such an outcome as she described would surely not be obtained easily.

Colin hesitated, but had to ask. "What, precisely, do you have in mind?"

Lady Clara's eyes narrowed. "Before we can formulate a course of action, we must first discover what precisely it is that Wallace is currently after. Why was Abigail permitted to reenter your life, Lord Haverford, and what roles do Eliza and Timothy have to play in his plot?"

Frustration gripped Colin once more. "Those are questions only Abigail can answer for us."

"Precisely," Lady Clara answered him with a sly grin. "I believe it is time for a tête à tête with your old friend."

Chapter 16

Rain splattered the window as Abigail studied the faces passing on the street in front of her home. Her notion she was being watched had only increased since her run-in with her father. Yet for all her searching, she had seen no trace of him since. Two days had passed with Abigail refusing to leave the house, claiming she needed time for her bruises to fade. Eliza and Clara had given her a day to recover, calling on her today to see how she fared. In the faint reflection of the window, Abigail could see the bruising on her face, but it was the frightened look in her eyes which struck her the most. How she hated being afraid.

"You ought to sit down," Clara instructed. "You are quite safe, I am certain. That horrible man has no reach here, not with Mr. Morgan to protect you."

With a sigh, Abigail returned to her chair. "I apologize for my melancholic air. It has been a trying few days."

Tea had been served previously, and she picked up her cup and sipped the tepid liquid.

Eliza's face drooped, her anguish quite readable. "I am the one who ought to apologize. I never should have left you that night, alone with that man. I had every intention of sending Clara to fetch you. Mrs. Fairbanks cornered me when I reentered the ballroom, and I quite forgot what I was about."

"Truly," Clara said. "Eliza has not stopped lamenting it since."

"You seemed to know him, so I never dreamed that he would hurt you so." Eliza's eyes filled with tears.

"Stop!" The sight of Eliza's remorse had weighed heavier on Abigail than the wrath of her father. "You are not to blame. You can believe I have received worse. This is all my fault, and I ought to have foreseen it."

Eliza's face clouded in confusion. "Whatever do you mean?" Her hand found Eliza's, placing gentle pressure upon her skin. "He has done this before?" A gasp. "In London, when we met. I see from your face I am correct. Doctor Rogers suspected, though I could not fathom such a thing. Oh, Abigail, what you have been through!" Tears of compassion coursed, unheeded, down her cheeks.

Abigail searched for the right words. Naivete had led her to the erroneous assumption that her life had changed, that the Morgans could protect her. She could no longer ignore what was going on around her. It was time to take responsibility for her own actions.

Her shoulders straightened, and she found the strength to continue. "It is not fair. You, the Morgans. All of you have a right to know the truth."

She turned to face the woman she had wronged, if only through false intentions, drawing on strength of character that she had not known she possessed. "I cannot continue like this. I am not the person they, or you, think me to be."

Eliza released Abigail's hand, drawing into herself as if awaiting a blow. Yet she patiently waited for Abigail to continue.

"I did not go to Edgemont to convalesce, nor to provide you with companionship during your family's absence, as you had so generously invited." Tears of relief trickled down her face as she shed her trickery and her voice grew stronger with every word. "My father sent me to rob you."

An inexplicable smile grew on Clara's face. "And now we come to it."

Confused by the comment, Abigail did not acknowledge it. Instead, she continued speaking to Eliza who sat mute in her seat. "I was sent to draw near to you, to gain your trust, and to find a way to steal your jewels."

Eliza wiped her face dry with a handkerchief, the time for crying apparently having ended. Finally, she spoke. "And did you succeed?"

Momentarily speechless at the lack of condemnation in the lady's voice, Abigail could only stare as she shook her head. Clara settled further into her chair, an amused expression on her face, as if she were witnessing a theatrical comedy rather than Abigail's new life crumbling at her feet.

"I thought not," Eliza said with satisfaction, a look of shared secrets passing between her and her sister. "My dear, we all suspected you arrived with ulterior motives. Perhaps not from the beginning, yet once Colin appeared and your identity was uncovered, we guessed something was amiss. It has proven fortuitous that you came, however. Not only have you been reunited with Colin, but also with your lost family!"

Abigail shifted uncomfortably. Did Eliza not understand? Where was the condemnation? The censure? The loathing?

"My dear," the lady continued softly. "I will not judge you on what you *might* have done. We are each of us capable of committing heinous misdeeds, yet it is not that upon which we are tried and sentenced. It is only our true actions that define who we truly are." She once again took Abigail by the hand. "You have confessed to me, yet you are guilty of no crime."

Abigail's head whirled with Eliza's pronouncement. Was she not to be cut? Disgraced? Humiliated? Was such magnanimity to be trusted?

"Abigail," Eliza said with a gentle squeeze of her hand, "I can see that you doubt my word. Truth be told, I would doubt it as well. Yet I do not regret it. As I have said before, you have my friendship. Now, what you do with that is up to you, although I would hope you will take this as proof that not all people are villains, and that you are worthy of so much more than you have known until now."

Abigail's heart beat painfully in her chest. Never had she been treated with such unending kindness. Staring at Eliza through eyes once again filled with tears left the lady appearing more as a mirage than a corporeal being. Perhaps she truly was an angel, as Abigail had previously thought, although the pressure applied to her hand testified to the contrary.

Wiping her eyes inelegantly with her sleeve, she felt like a child once more. "I do not know how to respond, my lady. I had thought to be cast aside."

"Oh, nonsense." Eliza laughed with a dismissive wave of her hand. "A true friend is too hard to come by within the *ton.* I will not lose one over such trivial matters."

"Neither of us wish to lose your friendship," Clara said. "Besides, this is the most excitement I have ever known during a Season. It makes me feel as if we are, each of us, heroines in one of those disgraceful novels Mother refuses to allow me to read."

Eliza laughed as if none of this mattered, causing Abigail to wonder if she was indeed placing too much importance on trifles. Yet what could be more vital than one's own moral character?

"Your forgiveness means more to me than I can possibly say." Abigail's voice cracked, further revealing her emotion.

"Then do not try. Let us put this behind us."

Clara leaned forward, a solemn expression replacing her smile. "Not quite, Eliza. Abigail's father has turned up once…"

"Twice," Abigail corrected. "The night I swooned at the ballet, it was from seeing him."

Understanding flashed in Clara's eyes and she nodded. "Twice now. What is to prevent him from coming for her once more?"

Clara voicing Abigail's own fears caused Abigail to take to her feet once more. "There is nothing to be done. Running or hiding are not options. I have attempted that before. He found me when I fled to London before, and he has found me now. He will find me the next time. He will always find me."

The Morgans could not possibly keep her protected at all times. Her father, or one of his henchmen, were bound to snatch her at some point. A woman might be disposed of with little to no notice in any back alley in this city, or even within the River Thames. The thought sent a shiver down Abigail's spine.

"What is it that he wants?" Clara asked. "You are no longer a guest in Eliza's home. What does he want of you now? You are of age. If you do not wish to associate with him, he can hardly force your hand."

Abigail may have been naive, but Clara had been completely sheltered. The lady knew nothing of the horrors a man such as her father could rain down upon all of their heads, Abigail's current bruising notwithstanding.

"He can, and he would not think twice about doing so." The rain had slowed outside and Abigail's view out the window cleared.

"He wants my jewels?" Eliza asked. "Could we possibly have some counterfeit pieces made?"

Abigail shook her head. "As angry as he was with me for coming to London, that is nothing to what he would do should he find me attempting to deceive him. Besides, he has been about his business for so long, it is likely he would recognize them as forgeries."

"What would your father do with the jewels, were he to get his hands on them?" Clara asked.

"I do not know what you mean."

"Would he sell them to the highest bidder? Or does he wish to gift them to you, his only daughter?" Abigail scoffed at the idea.

"No?" Clara asked thoughtfully. "He does not strike me as the sentimental sort, either. Would he then give them to creditors as a means of paying his debts?"

"I truthfully could not say. He would never include me in such decisions." Even as she answered, Abigail imagined she could see the wheels turning inside Clara's imagination, yet what her friend was formulating was anyone's guess.

"Being in possession of jewels stolen from the Marchioness Bedford is not itself an enviable position," Clara went on. "I would venture to guess that your father will be keen to rid himself of them nearly as soon as he receives them."

"'Receives them,'" Abigail repeated. "You cannot seriously be suggesting..."

A broad smile crept up Clara's face and she beamed, looking first at Abigail, then to Eliza.

"I am suggesting we give him what he wants. Eliza, we will give him your jewels."

"That is not necessary, my lady." How could Clara even suggest such a thing? "With your forgiveness, Eliza, I believe I shall take this opportunity as a fresh start. I will leave my father and my past life behind and move forward with the Morgans who seem quite intent upon furthering our acquaintance."

Clara rose, fervently pleading her case. "You said yourself that your father has found you now and he will find you again. What is to prevent him from coming after you once more? Abigail, what is to prevent him from inflicting some harm upon the Morgans? Your grandmother, your uncle! They wish only the best for you. Will you now place them in such danger?"

Abigail's legs shook beneath her as the reality of her situation became apparent. Clutching the window frame, she realized Clara's reasoning was sound. These people, who had so recently come into Abigail's life, already meant the world to her. She could not, in good conscience, place them in harm's way. Placing her hands on the cool glass before her, she wished to lay her face there as well, as the room felt too warm and close.

"As flippant as Clara is with my jewels," Eliza said, "I am of a mind to agree with her."

Abigail turned back, facing these mad sisters once more. "And what of your husband, Eliza? You may wear said jewelry, yet they are lawfully your husband's possessions. I doubt he would appreciate you so carelessly discarding them."

"Carelessly, my dear? Heavens no. This is not a decision I take lightly, nor is it one I intend to regret." Eliza straightened, a regal aura surrounding her person, and for the first time, Abigail saw the full potential this marchioness had to command those around her. "Let me be perfectly clear. This is not a gift, nor a loan. I offer these valuable pieces with the full expectation that they shall be returned to me being no worse for wear."

"Yes, yes. Of course, Eliza." Clara's smile returned and she retook her seat. "Now, is there anything more we need to know?"

Taking a deep breath, Abigail conceded defeat, although there was one thing she needed to verify once more. "We are yet friends, Eliza? Truly?"

Eliza, who had sat throughout the entirety of their exchange, now rose and approached Abigail, gazing at her intently. "Yes, my dear. I am indeed your friend. For now and always."

She drew strength from Eliza's sincerity. "There is more." Abigail hesitated only a moment before continuing. "My father has spies everywhere, including within your household." Both women's eyes grew wide as Abigail told them about the night at Edgemont when she was accosted outside her bedchamber.

For the first time, Abigail recognized fear on Eliza's face, having felt the emotion so often in her own life. Surprisingly, Abigail watched as that emotion turned to anger in the other woman.

Eliza's hands clenched and fire shot from her eyes. "All of this has been going on in my house, beneath our very noses?" For the first time Abigail saw fear enter Eliza's eyes. "And with my son in the house? This shall not stand! Immediately upon our return, we will find Timothy and inform him. He will know what to do."

One more thought lay heavy upon Abigail. "Please," she asked, looking from one lady to the next, "Colin cannot know anything is amiss. He is reckless and will surely wish to confront anyone involved, but he does not know my father like I do. You do not know him, or what he is capable of. It is not simply my life that hangs in the balance here. I will not be the cause of harm coming to any one of you!"

Clara looked back at her unflinching. Where did this woman's courage originate? Had her life been so completely without trial that she had no comprehension for the horrors evil men can bring?

Eliza took Abigail's hands in her own and spoke slowly, yet with authority. "Abigail, my husband is a marquess, and Colin is a viscount. As such, they are hardly simple targets for someone such as your father. They are not friendless, nor are they simple-minded. There are resources within their control. They will see Clara's plan through to fruition and we will all see justice done." Eliza placed a hand to Abigail's cheek, forcing their eye contact. "You have friends. You no longer need to carry this burden alone."

Chapter 17

The rumble of the carriage blended with the midday sounds of London, yet none of the cacophony penetrated Abigail's awareness. On her lap she carried a brown leather satchel, filled with riches beyond anything she had ever held. Hands shaking, she gripped the leather, feeling the outlines of the gems within. The thought of losing it weighed heavy on her shoulders. Her stomach heaved and she wished, not for the first time since this plot was conceived, that it was already over.

As if in answer to a silent prayer, the carriage slowed to a stop. Abigail jostled within as her uncle's footman disembarked and opened the door for her. The driver had halted down the street from the Grosvenor Gate entrance to Hyde Park, as per Abigail's instructions. The park was overflowing with people out to see and be seen on this sunny Sunday afternoon. Abigail had learned since her arrival for the Season that this was called the Fashionable Hour. Clara had planned this timing carefully, hoping with all of the other traffic, Abigail could enter unnoticed by any of the few acquaintances she had made since arriving in London.

Clutching the bundle close to her chest, Abigail made her way through the park, across the grassy expanse intersected by walking paths. Not wishing to be followed, she meandered from one path to the next, carefully avoiding eye contact with any passersby. She had arrived with ample time to spare before she was due to meet him, yet she fought the urge to speed her steps. The desire to have this rendezvous over and done with waged against her fear of the outcome, both clamoring for dominance.

When was the last time she had been so afraid? The memory came to mind almost instantly. The night her father had secreted her away from Stockwood House—Colin's ancestral home. That night had been the last time she had something of value to lose. Colin's friendship. And now she faced the possibility of losing him once more. If she failed, if her father saw through her, if she erred in some way... He would surely take his revenge upon the people she cared about most. Those she loved.

Her foot hit a rock causing her to stumble, the parcel falling from her grasp, the clinks from the jewelry ringing out as it landed a few paces before her. Her heart skipped a beat as a gentleman walking toward her stopped to retrieve it. How could she be so foolish? She had drawn attention to herself, and worse yet, to her bundle. If this gentleman opened the package, it would be evident something was amiss. No one who owned such pieces would be careless enough to take an easy stroll through the park with them in such a fashion.

The gentleman's eyes narrowed in suspicion. He must be feeling the shapes of the pieces through his gloves! Was he trying to place her, flipping through his memory to see if they had been introduced prior to this moment? Her jumbled thoughts ran on as the moment stretched into eternity, each seeming to be waiting for the another to proceed first.

At long last, the gentleman placed a smile on his face and, removing his hat, bowed. "I believe this belongs to you?" He stretched out toward her as he offered the package back.

She forced a shaky laugh. "Yes, I truly must be more careful." Fighting the urge to quickly snatch it back, she slowly took the offering. Never before had she been so grateful for society's rules of conduct as she was now. "As we have not been properly introduced, I will thank you, and be on my way."

Abigail moved around him, but was surprised when he turned along with her and matched her steps. She stopped once more, clutching the parcel so tight she was sure she would leave nail marks in the leather.

"I find myself hesitant to allow a young lady to continue roaming the park unattended," he said, and Abigail realized she now had a new fear to add to her list. The stranger made a point of looking her up and down, as if he were appraising horse flesh. Her skin prickled and she found it difficult to breathe.

Looking at her surroundings, she recalled the reason for her venturing out in midday as opposed to using the darkness to her advantage. When given an audience of strangers, one might be less likely to inflict bodily harm on another. Her father had come to mind at the time the details were being decided, yet it ought to be just as true now with this stranger.

"One would wonder," he continued, "where a young lady, such as yourself, would be headed on her own."

"Mr. Shelton," came a familiar voice from behind them. "I wonder at your being in Town this Season."

Turning along with the stranger, Abigail's heart skipped a beat to see Colin on his stallion, accompanied by Lord Bedford. Her fear doubled upon seeing the expressions of disgust upon both men's faces as they gazed down upon her companion. She had not spoken with Colin for several days and had not informed him nor Lord Bedford of this plot against her father. Had Eliza explained to her husband what they were about? Or would the men's displeasure be turned upon her next?

"Lord Bedford, Lord Haverford," Mr. Shelton snarled. "You know I am now the Earl of Gravestone. Proper decorum dictates that you refer to me as such."

Gravestone? Was this slimy specimen a relation of Lady Gravestone?

Abigail's surprise at such a revelation was overpowered by the shock of seeing anger immediately take over Lord Bedford's face. It was a reaction so far out of what Abigail had come to expect of him, that she would have laughed at the absurdity if it had not been altogether frightening. Mr. Shelton, or Lord Gravestone, or whatever his name was, took a few steps back with both Lord Bedford and Colin following to close the gap. This effectively left Abigail out of the circle of conversation and provided an easy escape as she slipped back into the throng of riders and pedestrians roaming the park along with them.

How long Colin would be held up by Mr. Shelton was anyone's guess, yet the men could still be heard as she retreated from them.

"You would speak of proper decorum?" Lord Bedford ground out. "After your conduct toward Lady Clara, you have no standing to lecture anyone on the finer points of being a gentleman."

"Timothy," Colin said, likely in an attempt to soothe his friend and avoid an all-out duel.

Abigail could hear no more as she moved further on her way. Continuing on the assumption that Eliza or Clara must have shared their plans with the men, and they would allow her to fulfill her purpose, she hurried to her rendezvous. Thankfully, she was now very near the agreed upon location, the very same place she had left past correspondence for her father.

Within a few moment's time, she saw the bulky frame of her father standing precisely where she expected. A myriad of emotions flooded her upon seeing him. As eager as she was to be rid of her burden, she yet could not believe she was about to hand over the marchioness's jewels to this man. Could such a plan as theirs truly be successful? Or would this be the last any of them saw of this wealth? The idea of being incarcerated within debtors' prison flashed just as her father turned in her direction.

His eyes trained upon the package in her hands. A strange softening overtook his features, and an inexplicable expression of sadness came over him. "This is it?" he asked, indicating her burden.

"Father, you realize…" she began, only to be silenced with a look from him.

"Do not speak," he growled. "Not now."

Could she simply turn back and return to the relative safety of the Morgan's townhouse? Every instinct in her body was telling her to flee to the comfort of Colin's arms, but neither of those actions could happen at this moment.

Abigail spared a glance behind her, searching the area where she had left Colin. He remained in the same place, his face pale as if registering shock. It was suddenly quite evident that the gentlemen had not been informed as to Clara's scheme, for Colin appeared as one seeing a ghost. His eyes continued to be locked on her father, and his shock quickly gave way to such rage she imagined she could feel it radiating off him, even at this distance. Lord Bedford remained beside Colin, still speaking with Mr. Shelton, or Lord Gravestone, whoever he was.

"Father, it is not safe to keep these out in the open like this." She pulled at her father's arm, attempting to gain his attention as he was solely focused on what he held in his hands.

Her father, at last wresting his eyes from his prize, motioned for Abigail to follow as he led her further into the copse of trees. Once out of sight of Colin and the other park patrons, her father signaled to a man who had been half hidden behind a tree. Abigail cursed herself for not taking notice of him as she walked. Now it was too late. Before she could take a breath to scream, the man had her around with a knife point pressed against the small of her back. She had proceeded directly into her father's trap.

"Scream and I will end you now," he said just loud enough for her to hear.

Yanking on her arm, he pulled her into the cover of the trees, out of view of the other park patrons. Her father followed, a satisfied smirk on his lips as he clearly fought the urge to open the parcel right then and there. They kept a healthy pace, her father paying her no more heed than he would a pebble beneath his feet.

"Father…" Abigail pleaded.

The man increased the pressure on the knife and Abigail bit down on her lower lip, fighting the need to cry out.

"I said no talking!" he hissed, pushing her to move even faster.

Abigail was certain he would not take kindly to hearing her correct him. And she did not doubt that he would absolutely kill her in front of her father, who would not object in the slightest.

As quickly as her mind could manage, she thought through her situation. Colin and Lord Bedford had surprised her with their presence and had saved her from the unwanted presence of a stranger. The jewels were yet in full view, and her father had not discarded her out of hand. For now, her best option was to do as she was told, so as not to draw out her father's ire. There was no doubt that her life fully depended upon his good graces.

Exiting the trees on the north end of the park, Abigail was led through a gate and out to the street and deposited within a waiting carriage, her father climbing in after her. The knife-wielding stranger climbed up to serve as driver. Abigail's fear of being alone with her father in such a confined place made her feel light-headed. Searching the area of the park visible through the carriage window she watched for any sign of Colin. Unfortunately, he could not be seen through the trees.

A slight rustle drew her attention back to her father who was now opening the parcel, pulling the jewels out one after another. He mumbled something too faint for her to make out, then looked up at her with a wicked grin.

"You have finally done it, Abby, my girl," he said, with an unusual and uncharacteristic pleasure. He placed the jewels back inside the case, closing it with a care she had never seen from him before. "I do not know how you did it, but you have shown you may be of some worth after all."

After the years of insults and slights, this small amount of praise brought a tear to Abigail's eye that she angrily swiped away. His approval ought not to bring about such longings for more. She knew what sort of man he was, for she had seen firsthand what a true man ought to be. The kindness, the strength and care that Colin exhibited was infinitely superior to any qualities her father possessed, yet she found she still cared for what her father thought of her.

Was she making a mistake? Was this entire plot ill-founded? Would she be able to forgive herself on the off chance that they were actually able to succeed? Her father would be stopped, imprisoned, punished for his multitude of crimes, and all by her hand. Would she be able to live with that?

"Y-you have what you wanted," she said, her voice quavering. "What will you do with it now?"

His eyes shot to hers as the carriage jostled to a halt. "They will be sold, and I will move on, as always."

There was no mention of her going with him. Had he simply neglected to include her, or was it a purposeful omission? Before she could ask, he had the door opened and was gone, entering the inn they had arrived at. Exiting the carriage herself, she looked up at the sign above the door reading *The Wobbly Sailor*. Where they were precisely, she had no idea, as they had moved away from the area of London she had begun to know.

Eyes of various layabouts followed her as she stood, unsure what to do with herself until her father's man joined her. Roughly grabbing her by the arm, he pulled her inside, heedless of the many eyes watching their spectacle.

"'Ello there," an older man greeted her from behind a counter, her father standing across from him.

"They are with me," her father stated flatly.

"Very good, sir," the man replied, then turned back to address Abigail and the man once more. "Yer father's room is up the stairs, three doors off the left. Or if'n you be 'ungry, you can seat yerself in the larger room there, and some food'll be brought in."

Had her father reserved only one room for the three of them? How could he expect her to share a room with another man? Her reputation, such as it was, would be completely ruined.

"Thank you," she said, turning toward the dining room he had indicated. As she left, she heard the man approach her father.

"I did as you said, now where is my coin?"

Breathing a sigh of relief, she realized this was likely all that man had signed up to do, and it would presumably be only herself and her father sharing a room this evening.

Upon entering the dining room, Abigail was assaulted by the smell of something unpleasant. Unfortunately, knowing the instability of her father's temper, she would be best served to take what food she was offered now, however unpalatable it may be, as it might be some time before the opportunity came once more.

Abigail found an empty table near the edge of the room and sat. After a few moments, her father joined her.

Finding some reserve of courage, she asked, "Was there a purpose to having me so carefully escorted here?"

"Simply to prevent you getting any ideas about not coming with me. I know how living that life can turn a person's head. I was simply looking out for you."

The false thoughtfulness made Abigail's stomach turn. Thinking it more likely that he did not wish her to alert

Bow Street of his presence, she chose not to bait him further while there were more urgent matters left to discuss.

"You mentioned selling the jewels, Father."

"What of it?" he growled.

"Since I have been associating with several people who have the means to purchase such things, I may have a lead on a buyer."

Rather than brushing her aside as he had in the past, her father actually seemed of a mind to listen. "Go on."

Keep your voice steady! "I overheard an older woman admiring the jewels when the marchioness wore them to the ball last week," she lied. "I think that if given the chance, she could be persuaded to buy them. There is no love lost between them, and I believe that she would love the chance to take something precious from Lady Bedford."

"Well, well, Abby. You certainly are full of surprises today." He leaned back in his chair. "I suppose you have not forgotten what the penalty of failure would be. You would not dare cross me now, would you, *daughter*?"

All of her strength went into her answer. "No, Father. You can trust me."

Chapter 18

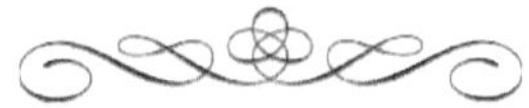

Colin slammed the door open as he stomped his way through his entryway into his study, Timothy at his heels. One thought resounded through him time and time again.

She is gone.

Seeing Abigail trembling before the likes of that smug little man, *Lord Gravestone* had been torture enough, and yet he had stood there and simply watched as Abigail entered the lion's den with her father. Immobilized by the shock of it all, he had moved to follow only to be stopped by Timothy. His friend had held him back, knowing by the time they could arrive where he had seen Abigail, they would be long gone. It galled Colin that Christopher Wallace could indeed do all he wished to his daughter.

And now she was gone, and Colin could blame no one but himself.

His shame gave way to anxiety greater than any he had previously known, and he feared he would never recover a sense of security after this. It had been one thing to lose Abigail in the past. He had been young, inexperienced, and completely taken by surprise. This time? Well, this time he had no one to blame but himself, and that was precisely what he was doing.

"Colin, slow down!" Timothy grabbed at Colin's arm, which he immediately shrugged off. "Take a breath."

The tone of voice employed by the aristocracy when they made demands was something that came innate to men such as Timothy, and he used it now. Colin was not certain whether he ought to be amused or affronted by such being directed his way. Looking at his friend, one who had stood by him during all those years of searching for Abigail, he could be neither.

Shrugging from his coat, he tossed the crumpled mess onto a spare chair set in the corner. He staggered under the weight of his cares, and slumped into the high-back chair behind his desk.

"You trust Abigail, do you not?" Timothy asked.

"Trust her?" Colin repeated. "Two weeks ago I would have answered whole-heartedly in the affirmative. After today? I am not so sure."

"Very well," Timothy relented. "You love her?"

Colin looked him in the eyes. "With every fiber of my being."

"Then you must trust her. Trust that she is doing what she feels is best, for her and for you."

Seeing the wisdom in what his friend was saying, Colin took a deep breath. "The older man with Abigail was her father."

"That much was evident," Timothy said as he settled deeper into his seat. "What of the other man?"

"I haven't the slightest idea. If we are lucky, Abigail most of all, he will prove to be merely hired muscle."

"Perhaps." Timothy shifted forward, elbows on his knees. "Where would they take her?"

"My man on Bow Street has been unable to locate Wallace's base of operation here in London. Wallace is too clever to remain in one place, though. It is my belief that he alters his location each time he ventures here."

Timothy cleared his throat, a look of utter sympathy on his face. "She is with her father, Colin," he said, mimicking what Colin had previously told himself. "He has every right to take her wherever he pleases. Perhaps it is time to let her go," he said kindly.

Huffing, Colin shrugged off the suggestion. "If I knew how to do that, I would have done so years ago."

A pause. "If that is the case, then perhaps we have not been asking the right questions." Timothy offered.

Colin rubbed at the scowl that seemed perpetual these days, forcing his brows to relax. "What do you mean?"

"One thing has persisted in bothering me. Did it ever strike you as odd the way she has spoken of her name?" Timothy asked.

Colin's frustration forced him from his chair. "Her name is Abigail Wallace," he said testily.

"Yes, that was the name you knew her by. Yet Eliza knew her as Abigail Newell, and now she is Abigail Morgan. We have always assumed that Christopher Wallace was her father's name as that is what he went by when in your father's employ. Yet, what if his nefarious actions began before he was your father's steward?"

"You are suggesting that Wallace was also a false name?" Colin could have kicked himself for his stupidity. None of his Bow Street contacts had ever suggested such a thing either, although they did not have a reputation for being clever. As it was, he strode quickly to the window, gazing at the mews behind the house. "I have been wholly focused on finding his current location that I have scarcely given thought to his life before I knew them."

"We need more information if we are to launch an investigation into his background. Where were they before entering into your father's employ?"

"I never thought to ask. At the time of their disappearance my father handled the investigation with the local magistrate. I was sent away to finish out my last term at Eton and was cut off from any additional information that he was able to glean before he passed."

Colin retook his seat and pulled a blank sheet of paper from the desk drawer. Writing quickly, he scrawled instructions for Duncan to begin researching Wallace using any possible aliases based on the types of crimes they knew him to be guilty of. All such unsolved crimes in any areas around the country that fit this criminal's mode of operation would also need to be investigated.

Moving quickly, he threw the door open and was unsurprised to find a footman awaiting his request. It was evident the household staff knew of his agitation upon returning home, and were prepared to meet his every need. Never before had he been so grateful for their superb assistance.

"See that this is delivered to Bow Street."

The footman gave a curt nod before disappearing down the corridor. Colin turned back to Timothy as he took his seat once more.

"Now," Timothy continued. "Why would Abigail be meeting her father in the park?"

An excellent question.

"From what I understand," Colin stated, "Eliza and Lady Clara paid her a visit yesterday. Do you know if that occurred?"

"If it did, I have yet to hear of it. Eliza got called away soon after her return, giving us little time to speak."

Releasing some of his frustrations gave way for Colin to think critically about the day's events. "And what was Abigail carrying?" he mused.

Timothy rose. "These are questions for my wife to answer. It is her day to receive visitors, so we know she will be at home. Perhaps we can catch a few minutes of her time in between visits."

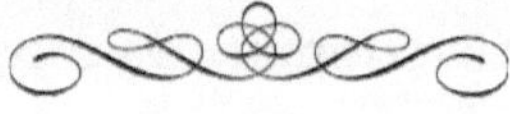

"Your jewels?" Timothy bellowed.

The three of them now stood in Timothy's library. The men had been obliged to wait three quarters of an hour for Eliza's visitors to leave. Colin had stewed with his questions as he paced, while Timothy caught up on some reading. How the man could be so calm in the face of his friend's turmoil was a mystery. And from what Colin could tell, the largest mystery until now had been what was carried within Abigail's parcel.

Eliza shrunk back slightly in the face of her husband's fury. Colin could hardly blame the woman. He had known Timothy for nearly fifteen years, and never once in all that time had the man shown such temper.

"I-I hardly think it worth working yourself up…"

Colin could hear her attempt at a soothing tone of voice, yet it came out stumbling and frail, like a child caught in a lie.

"You hardly think?" Timothy repeated, eyes wide.

Colin took a step nearer his friend, and repeated Timothy's earlier directive. "Timothy, take a breath. Think about this lest you say something you regret."

Timothy's face reddened. "I regret? Ha!" Regardless, he took several deep breaths before continuing. "Eliza," he said carefully, desperation creeping into his voice. "Those jewels have been in my family for generations. Beyond that, they belonged to my mother. How could you discard them so readily?"

"They are hardly discarded," she answered, her voice gaining strength. It was evident she felt she had acted in the right. "I gave them freely, yes. However, I did so to help a friend. You would have done the same had you been here."

"I fail to see how this helps Abigail," Colin interjected, drawing both gazes. Had they forgotten he was here?

"Do you?" Timothy asked incredulously. "Those jewels, sold to the appropriate dealer, would reasonably set a man up for three lifetimes! It would cost a small fortune for me to replace them, not to mention the sentimentality they hold for me. I grew to manhood seeing my mother wear them, and now I see them adorn my own wife."

Eliza's face paled. "I had not considered…"

Timothy seemed to fold into himself, slouching most unlike his usual impeccable stature, and spoke as though he was alone. "Perhaps they can yet be salvaged if I go now to Bow Street and report it as a theft."

"No," Eliza said, taking Timothy's hand in hers. "I did not give them to Abigail with no thought of them being returned. Clara has formed a plan for us to regain the jewels and be done with Christopher Wallace for good. Abigail and I were simply following our portions of the scheme."

"Clara has a plan?" Timothy asked, his eyes nearly popping from their sockets. "You are simply following your sister's lead? Your sister, who barely has more experience in life than a newly-presented debutante?"

Eliza's eyes lit with her own fire and Timothy took a step back. "Do not dare speak ill of my sister! There are more ways than one in this life to sow seeds of misery, and one as well read as she would have no end to ideas of how I can turn your life into…"

Colin, fearing for his own safety, felt honor bound to step in. "Eliza, I am certain Timothy did not intent to malign Lady Clara. This is not the concern of either of you. It is my duty to set this right. It is, after all, my trespass against you both. Were it not for my blindness regarding Abigail, you would not be in such a position." He turned back to his friend. "Timothy, if you go to Bow Street now, you know it will soon come to light that your wife freely gave that wealth to a criminal. She will be judged by the *ton*, ridiculed for her naivete. Every eye will be drawn to the bareness of her neck, the lack of earbobs. You have good cause to be angry now, yet do you truly wish for her to be subject to such scrutiny?"

Timothy turned to consider his wife, and Colin witnessed the softening around his eyes that answered those questions.

"You have two days."

Colin took a breath. "I will begin with a visit with Lady Clara to hear her explanation."

Colin stared at Eliza, standing beside Timothy's desk, appearing a shell of the happy woman he knew. Regret filled him as he felt the responsibility of reducing her to such a state. Had he irrevocably altered the relationship of his dearest friends? Would his efforts towards Abigail come with a cost too high to pay?

Chapter 19

Abigail sat quaking beneath her cloak, half hidden at the corner table of the pub's great room. Her father insisted upon conducting his business in the midst of large groups of people, as he was convinced it added an air of legitimacy to his dealings. She suspected, in truth, it had more to do with his pride, thinking himself clever enough to fool anyone. And within this rowdy tavern there were a fair amount of drunken louts and wanton women who would not be too difficult to outwit.

Looking at him now, across the small table, she shivered to her core. He had kept this aspect of his life apart from her, disdainfully maintaining that business was no place for a woman. He had only allowed her into this particular assignment regarding the marchioness and her jewels. She could not leave this evening's events to chance, nor could she sit demurely somewhere waiting for news of what had transpired.

A crash sounded behind the counter, startling Abigail and causing half the room's inhabitants to search for the cause. Behind the counter, one of the barmaids had dropped a tray of full tankards, drawing the disapproval of the owner who had several harsh things to say in response that could just be heard over the revelry of the patrons. Abigail's sympathy flew to the girl who was little more than a child. Memories of being the recipient of her father's wrath flashed before her as she clung to her seat to stop herself from rising in defense of the girl. Such an act would hardly keep her out of the notice of others. Nor would it gain her any sympathy from her father.

"Your buyer is late," her father grumbled. His eyes were stormy and she could feel the intensity radiating off his taut muscles. She knew what would happen if everything did not go according to their design, or at least what would happen to her. He had shown no hesitation in reminding her several times leading up to this meeting.

"S-she will be here," she answered, pulling at a stray thread on her skirt in her anxiousness. Even though she had been brought up in this life, she knew she would never adapt to its demands. It was just as well she had made this move to rebel against it.

Looking over her father's shoulder, she caught the eye of a patron at the next table. Did he just wink at her? She averted her eyes, pulled the hood of her cloak down closer to her cheeks, and wished she could disappear within it. What she would not give to have this ordeal finished. She had scarcely taken a moment to consider what she would do after tonight, focusing all her attention on this one encounter and ensuring all the other players were prepared. Having no way to arrange an actual meeting with anyone else, she had sent notes, similar to those she had sent to her father in the past, detailing what needed to be done.

She took a moment now to consider her uncle Peter's disapproval over her absence of the past two days. What must he think of her? How could she hope to return to him and her grandmother? They had trusted her, provided for her, loved her even, had welcomed her into their home and presented her to the *ton.* And she had repaid their kindnesses by vanishing with no warning or explanation. It was likely they would wash their hands of her, offering to support her no longer. And if she was successful tonight, she would no longer need to fear her father, which meant she would no longer be able to count on him for support, either. It seemed like a double-edged sword, as it were.

A small ruckus near the door drew Abigail's attention. An old crone of a woman was hobbling toward their table, a cane rhythmically thumping with every other step. She stood hunched over, a gray cloak with moth-eaten holes draped over a deforming hump rising from her back. The woman's face was shadowed by a mop of greasy grey hair that hung limply before her, except when it moved with each exhale. Surprisingly, the aging woman's teeth shone out, completely intact and incongruous with the rest of the image.

Abigail pinched her legs to keep herself from laughing out, and stole a glance back at her father. Would he know? Was this entire enterprise doomed before it began?

"Ah, now. Ah, now," the woman rasped, indicating those she passed as she hobbled in Abigail's direction. "No need to rise, all yous noble gentlimens. Mys beauty tis nothin' to halt the appetite, surely. I's but a 'umble servant, I is." Taking her cane up in her hand, the woman rapped it smartly on the table top, assuring Abigail's father's attention. As if they could possibly be looking at anything else in the room.

Abigail cleared her throat. "You are Mrs. Morley, I presume?" She had chosen to use the name of Colin's trusted valet knowing her father would not recognize it.

"Right you is, miss, and might I say what a lovely young thing you is." The woman turned to Abigail's father with a glint in her eyes. "You must be right proud of this 'un then. Beauty like that can't be bought, now can it?" She sat down, pulling her chair so close to Abigail's father that he attempted to back up. The effort merely leaned his chair back on its hind legs, and he had to grab at the table to prevent himself from falling. Righting himself, he straightened the worn coat he wore and attempted to mask his distaste for their new companion.

"Mrs. Morley, might I present my father, Mr. Christopher..." Abigail trailed off at the glare her father sent her as she realized too late her mistake. He had warned her beforehand not to use his name. The hatred blazing from his eyes solidified her resolve to see this through to the end.

"We are not here to observe the niceties of polite society," her father growled out. "You have brought payment?"

"Right I did," the crone agreed, seeming unconcerned with the tension flooding the area. "Right I did, yet I must see them goods 'afor I goes payin' for nothin'."

Abigail's father signaled the barmaid for more drinks. "Business ought not be done too hastily, now. Perhaps you would like a little refreshment first?"

"Aye, I see through your games, young man," the old woman answered with a cackle. "You think if I were to get a bit tipsy you could take more of me money, is that it?" She wagged a finger at him. "Well, I tells you, I can 'old me liquor with the best of the Queen's Navy, I can. Can you say the same, I wonder? As 'tis, I never say no to a nice pint."

Her father turned an incredulous glance her way. Luckily, before he could formulate anything to say about their companion's odd conversation, the barmaid arrived, struggling under her heavy-laden tray, the tankards' contents sloshing over the edges.

"Now," the crone said, grabbing a tankard from the young girl and taking a large swig, "tell me, where'd you lot come by such fine treasure, eh? And how's I to know the proper owners won't come callin' at me mistress's door?"

"Well now," her father said. "I see you have got some brains to go along with your...considerable life experience. This may seem difficult to believe, however...I am the proper owner."

Abigail stared at her father. She knew him to be a liar, yet he was typically more discreet than this. He had taught her that the best falsehoods contain a bit of truth, and to only lie about what was absolutely necessary to achieve one's purpose. Why would he lie about something so blatantly false as himself being the rightful owner of such fine pieces of jewelry? It did not make any sense.

"And I's the queen of the realm," the crone cackled. "Go on, *me lordship*, and spin us another yarn."

"It is true!" Abigail's father hit the table with his open palm and jumped to his feet. Glancing around the room, he immediately calmed himself and retook his seat. Abigail could only stare in disbelief, wondering if perhaps the man had gone mad. Up until now the only bouts of temper she had witnessed from him had been directed at herself or, once upon a time, her mother. It was a bit of a relief to have his ire directed toward another, and to one who seemed absolutely capable of facing it.

Upon sitting once more her father took a long draft of his ale, then wiped his arm across his mouth, sopping up some of the liquid that had dribbled down his chin. Abigail had never seen her father in such a state. He seemed utterly upended, truly unpredictable. A feeling of dread replaced her earlier relief and settled over her shoulders like an old enemy returned from the dead. She could not help the shuddering chill that crept over her.

A warm weight pressed down on her leg under the table, unseen by her father. Abigail snatched it in both her hands and put all her unspoken emotions into the tightness of her grip. The old crone looked into her eyes and Abigail was soothed by the calmness she saw within their grey depths, so like her own in color, yet infinitely more capable of bringing her peace.

Colin was here.

No longer wishing to laugh at his disguise, she now felt supreme gratitude. Colin's fingers threaded through hers and once more she had to suppress a laugh as he winked at her, then turned his attention back to her father who had begun speaking. Her father was sure to notice if they kept gazing at one another in such a manner.

"I will admit to no ownership for the majority of the pieces," he was saying in a more controlled tone of voice as he pulled a bundle out from a satchel at his feet. "Yet there is one for which I was responsible for procuring." Opening the bundle, he unfolded a length of fabric, affording Colin a quick glance at its contents before picking one small item out and replacing the lot within the satchel. Abigail watched as Colin, releasing her hand, signaled something to the man she had noticed looking her way earlier. Her father quickly drew her attention once more as he held up a small ring with a lone ruby expertly placed in a setting of tiny diamonds. The gems were small, yet the overall craftsmanship was breathtaking. "I commissioned this to be crafted twenty-five years ago."

"How…?" Abigail could not formulate a proper question as so many fluttered through her mind.

"How could something I own come to be in the possession of a marchioness?" her father provided the question for her. "The late marchioness was a lovely woman. Never had I seen such beauty. She stole my heart the moment we met, treating me like an equal, not some garbage to be trod underfoot." A faraway look entered his eyes. "She was the only woman I ever truly loved."

Abigail's stomach lurched. She had suspected he had not loved her mother, yet to have him admit such a thing so openly and without shame... and before a complete stranger no less.

Anger flashed through his eyes once more. "Made me believe she loved me in return. Oh, the plans I made, the adventures we would have had. I would have gone anywhere, done anything, been anyone for her. I had this ring made for her, and after several weeks, worked up the courage to ask for her hand. No need to ask her father, as I knew his answer would be a resounding no. We would have had to elope, go to Gretna Green. Yet when I spoke to her, she would have nothing to do with the idea! She spoke only of her meeting the *delightful Marquess of Bedford.* She had taken me for granted. I was her plaything, a delightful diversion. He turned her head with thoughts of climbing further up the social hierarchy."

Of course it could have nothing to do with wishing to know where one's next meal is coming from, thought Abigail. He always did have the propensity to blame others for his own failings. Never had he been one to admit to any weakness or fault within his own character.

"I left as quickly as possible, not thinking of the ring she still held in her hands. She wounded me deeply, yet I had the final triumph. I tricked her silly friend into running away with me instead. I took her favorite companion, and she took my ring. She was welcome to keep it, but the wife of the marquess' son is not. When I learned that my own daughter had befriended that woman, I realized it was my chance to retrieve it. Gratefully, my useless daughter has proven to be slightly more adept than I had supposed."

Abigail saw Colin's jaw clench at the insult, and before she could signal for him to remain calm, he had leapt from his seat, the charade at an end. Tearing the cloak and wig from his head in one swift motion, he revealed his true identity. Abigail knew he held himself from attacking her father by the slightest thread of self-control, and for that she loved him more.

Her father was slower to react; perhaps his years were finally beginning to catch up to him. Horrified, he threw himself back, away from Colin, and attempted to rise. The shock on his face brought a smile to Abigail's at finding himself restricted by four hands clamping down on his shoulders and arms from behind.

"Bind him well, Duncan," Colin said to one of the men.

"What? What is this?" Abigail's father yelled, looking up at his captors, likely assessing his chances of escape. Holding him were two men Abigail did not recognize, but knew must be trusted friends of Colin's. One of them took out a length of rope from under his cloak and began to tie her father's wrists together.

"This," Abigail said as she leaned back in her seat, flooded with relief, "is the end, Father. We are done. Finished with this business of yours."

As she spoke, the man Colin had signaled earlier approached, calmly reached down into her father's satchel, and removed the stolen items within. Upon closer inspection, she quickly recognized Lord Bedford in yet another disguise.

"It is unfortunate that you feel such ownership, Mr. Wallace," Lord Bedford said. "As you freely admitted, you presented this," he picked the ring up from where it had fallen on the table, "to my mother as a gift. Once that was done, the ownership transferred legally to my mother to be passed down as she saw fit. I do hope that time spent in prison will convince you of that fact, as the years between then and now have not."

"You, *daughter*?" her father hissed. "This is all your doing? After all I have done for you, all I have given you, you think to betray me? And for what? Tell me you do not still have your cap set for this one!" He indicated Colin with a twitch of his head. "I took you away from him to spare you the same heartache I had experienced! People in their positions cannot be trusted! They will use you ill, and send you packing when they are finished, just as I was discarded." Apparently seeing that his words had no effect on Abigail, he tried a new tactic to illicit a response. "You will be ruined," he sneered. "No one will want you once the viscount is through. Men can recover from such dalliances. Women cannot."

Abigail's gaze flicked to Colin for only a moment before returning to her father. Her spine straightened and her voice found strength. "Colin would never, *I* would never, be caught in such a disreputable predicament. And as to trust, Father?" she asked. "It is you who cannot be trusted. This man has done more for me during our few interactions than you have done my entire lifetime. I will go to my grave knowing there is kindness in the world, that not all men are as selfish and self-serving as you, and that love can conquer the darkest demons and heal the broken heart."

Now she had begun, she found herself with a multitude of things she wished to say. "Yet it is not for him that I have done this." She laughed without mirth. "No, this was for me. For I will never again be beholden to one such as you. I will no longer allow myself to be downtrodden, forced to do the bidding of another regardless of the echoes of my conscience."

"You think you are better than this? Better than your own father?" Her father laughed, not willing to let her be. "No one will welcome a thief into their house. You will have nowhere to go. No one to care for you. *You* are the one who took that jewelry—not I." He looked up at his captors once more, pleading with them. "She is who you want. I have done nothing!"

"Nothing but attempt to sell what does not belong to you," Colin said. He had wiped his face with a handkerchief, removing additional aspects of his disguise. "You call emptying half of my father's coffers nothing? These men from Bow Street have my report on what you stole from him as well. And now that you are apprehended, I have every confidence that more of your crimes will quickly be discovered."

"I do not understand," he repeated, turning his eyes upon Abigail who saw the fear in them. "What do you gain from this?"

Was it not obvious?

"I gain," she said as she slowly stood, rising above him as she had feared to do all her life, "a measure of peace."

Chapter 20

Abigail's father continued to yell and rant as the men restraining him escorted him out of the room. For the first time since the confrontation began, Abigail became aware of the many sets of eyes trained in her direction. It dawned on her then, that not every person in the room had been agents of Colin's, nor had they disappeared at the first sign of conflict. That, combined with the shock of what had transpired, caused her legs to quake and she sat down once more.

Colin, who had remained at her side, knelt and raised a hand to her forehead. "Are you well? Should I send for a doctor?"

His thoughtfulness at a time such as this endeared him to her, and she smiled softly. "There is no need. I am merely tired." Thinking of when she could sleep brought to mind that she knew not where she would do so. Her father's words came back to her. *You have nowhere to go. No one to care for you.* Feeling the truth of his words, she felt the blood drain from her head as panic replaced her relief.

The marquess seemed to notice. "Colin, we ought to be seeing your lady home."

Abigail resisted Colin pulling on her arm, attempting to help her stand. "That is thoughtful of you, my lord. Unfortunately, I have no home to go back to. My uncle Peter is sure to cast me out with my absence the past several days."

Lord Bedford's eyes filled with a knowing mischief, and he took the seat vacated by her father and said kindly, "I misspoke, forgive me. I, of course, meant my home, Miss Morgan. Lady Clara sent a message to your uncle informing him that you would be spending a few days with her and my wife, and requested he send some of your things round to our townhouse. Mr. Morgan has had no cause to worry over your absence."

Abigail looked at the man, disbelieving. "You cannot truly mean to welcome me back? After everything that I have taken from you?"

"What have you taken?" he asked, even as he rolled up the items once more and tucked them within a satchel he had apparently brought along with him. "From what I understand, these were freely loaned to you by my wife.

I would be quite put out to find that she told me a falsehood."

"I suppose she did do that," Abigail admitted. "Loan them to me, I mean. Yet what of..."

"Abigail," Colin interjected. "Do not dig yourself a hole you do not know a way out of. Timothy knows more than he lets on, and you have nothing that needs be explained tonight. You are not the only person who is tired. You will stay the night at Timothy's home, only because it would be disreputable for you to stay at mine. And on the morrow, you shall be returned to your uncle's care."

Rarely had Abigail witnessed Colin taking such a firm line on what needed to be done that she was inclined to submit to him without further protest. Before she could summon any response, however, the marquess leaned over the table toward her.

"Before we all retire for the evening, there is yet one question I would ask."

Abigail's heart stood still once more, unsure what the marquess could be thinking of. The serious timbre of the man's voice brought to mind all of Abigail's trespasses against him and his wife. "My lord, first I must apologize..."

Soft chuckling sounded throughout the enclosed space. "There is no need, Abigail. Might I call you that?"

"Of course," she answered. "After all you have done for me, it certainly makes sense for you to use my Christian name."

"I thank you. To be completely honest, as I am certain we shall always be with one another moving forward," he said pointedly, "I have thought of you as Abigail for many years now. Colin has forever referred to you as such and it has been quite inconvenient for me to always remember your current name of choice. That said, might I ask out of sheer curiosity, what is your true surname?"

The question took Abigail by surprise. Having given pseudonyms for herself for so many years, she rarely thought much on her legal name. It came to her now, thought the realization that she need not hide it gave her no comfort. It would forever feel tainted as it was irrevocably tied to the man who bestowed it. A quick glance at Colin proved his interest in her answer as well.

"It is Flores, my lord." She shifted uncomfortably, never having offered such information. "Abigail Flores. My father's ancestors were of Spanish origin, I believe. There is very little I know about my heritage, however, and I believe that I shall continue to presume upon my grandmother's generosity and use of the name Morgan, at least for now."

Smiling knowingly, he answered, "I believe that is wise."

Standing, she dipped a curtsy to the marquess. "I am grateful for your hospitality, my lord."

She allowed Colin to see her out the same way her father had been taken. Colin held her elbow as if he worried she would break, and her heart did just a little as a realization struck her.

"You have now righted the wrong my father did to yours," she said as they exited into the full darkness of night, her eyes fighting to adjust to the sudden absence of light. Her father and his captors were nowhere to be seen, as they must have immediately left for Newgate. "I suppose all those years of searching were not in vain."

"Vain?" Colin halted, then taking a firmer hold on her, pulled her further into the shadows. Tenderly cupping her head in his hands, he whispered, "Not for one moment of the rest of my life shall I ever regret that time. For it is what allowed me to find you."

He leaned nearer, and Abigail felt his breath on her nose. The love she heard in his voice nearly overwhelmed her with gratitude and adoration of him. Rising up, she met his lips with hers. Unlike their prior kiss, this one was slow and gentle, exploratory and soft. Their bodies seemed to merge together, as their union grew. After so many years of feeling lost and afraid, Abigail released herself into the care of another. He had come to her rescue with no thought of himself, nor his reputation. Trust had never come easily for her, yet she would give over her entire future to this man if he asked for it.

"I did not anticipate this being the setting for this," Colin said with a quick look around them. Stepping back, he placed a little space between them, yet kept hold of her arms. "However, I find I can wait no longer. You will never know the desperation I felt the morning I woke up all those years ago to find you had gone. My poor mother never did understand my hesitancy at showing the slightest interest toward any other woman, yet she loved me enough to indulge me. She passed, never seeing me truly happy in all that time."

Abigail opened her mouth to offer her condolences, and Colin raised a hand to halt her speaking, and he continued. "I do not say this to imply you ought to feel guilty for leaving, but rather to demonstrate the depths of my regard for you. I have never hidden nor shied away from those emotions. You are constantly at the forefront of my thoughts, and I cannot bear the idea of being parted from you even a day longer. Abigail Flores—

Egerton—Wallace—Newell—Morgan," he said with a wink, "will you consent to spend the rest of your life with me?"

Tears formed in Abigail's eyes as she reached up to brush his unruly hair from his eyes. "I have tried to live each moment with you as if it was our last, never knowing when I would be torn from your side once more. That idea alone has frightened me more than any unkindness from my father ever could. I have loved you since I was fourteen years old and I saw you running on the beach, having secreted from your home in the middle of the night. Even then, you never had nefarious intentions."

She smiled, the perfection of sharing her feelings after all these years nearly overwhelming her. "All you wished for was to be happy and increase the happiness of those around you. I cannot think of anything in this world that would bring me greater joy than to remain with you, always. Yes, of course I will spend my life with you, as anything less is simply unthinkable."

Colin grinned as he had never grinned before. It was the type of smile that made one's cheeks hurt after a while, and he knew this feeling would linger. He leaned in and kissed her once more.

The moment was cut short by a throat clearing nearby. Abigail, pinned between Colin and the wall of the pub, could not withdraw, and Colin was slow to move away. His hands ran smoothly down her arms until he focused on one hand and pulled it through his arm. Thus connected, he escorted her to the marquess's carriage which had been brought round, while the marquess waited for her to climb in.

"I do not know how I can ever thank you," Abigail said, looking between the two men. She was brimming with joy and peace such as she had never before known. "Both of you have assisted me well beyond what I deserve. If ever there is some way that I can repay you, by all means, let me know it."

"I am certain I will think up something," Colin said with a sly grin.

Timothy took her free hand to assist her into the carriage. "Leave her be, Colin. What she is in need of now is a solid night's sleep." He glanced back at his friend as he took his own seat across from Abigail. With a smile he added, "You may call on her on the morrow."

"You may count upon it, Timothy. You may indeed count upon it." With another smile, Colin closed the door and hit the side of the carriage signaling to the driver.

The carriage began its journey out of the seedy outskirts of London back to the clean streets of Mayfair. Rocking with the vehicle, Abigail was overcome with fatigue. The events of the past few days, combined with little rest, made her eyelids heavy and she forced back a yawn.

Timothy leaned back; his face once more hidden from view by shadows. "Now, you may close your eyes until we arrive, if you wish. It has been an excessively long evening."

Abigail did just that. The images that began floating through her mind were ones of happiness and contentment, far different than what would have come even a day before.

Flowers danced around her as she strolled through a crowded ballroom. Faces were faint until she came upon a group of her friends. They were all there, all the friends she had made over the past few months. And in the forefront of them all stood Colin, larger than life, his infectious smile lighting the room. Gazing down at her, as if she was his whole world, he took her hands in his and they began waltzing with the other couples. And then the others vanished and it was Colin and her, alone.

Knowing this to be a simple fantasy, Abigail could not hide her smile, and she was grateful for the darkness surrounding her. Her smile only grew as she suddenly realized that now such a dream could become reality. With her father no longer controlling her life, she could enjoy her time with her new family and all of the experiences that would come with it. And soon she would be forever united with Colin, the greatest man she had ever known.

Her smile broadened, and she thought she might never lose her smile again.

Epilogue

Colin strolled leisurely through Hyde Park with his wife at his side. A month had passed since their prior visit within these boundaries, though it seemed a lifetime ago as so much had taken place since then. This time Abigail was beside him, well within his reach, and he was happy beyond compare.

Her father was now safely tucked away within the walls of Newgate Prison awaiting trial. Colin's men on Bow Street had linked several more robberies to Christopher Flores's long list of crimes. His trial had not as yet been scheduled, although with no one speaking on his behalf, it was as good as over.

The single remaining variable that Abigail cared for was his sentencing. Colin, who was receiving constant updates from his various contacts, knew there were three likely scenarios. First, Christopher would remain in Newgate for the rest of his days. Second, he would be hung. Or third, and this was the most likely scenario, he would be exiled to the inhospitable reaches of Botany

Bay. Colin knew which option he would prefer, yet for Abigail's sake he would never utter the words aloud. He knew she longed for her father to be far away from herself, though she was too generous a soul to wish for any man's ultimate demise.

"I have been thinking of our time together," Abigail said, breaking the comfortable silence between them. "I cannot think when I have been so content."

"Indeed," he murmured. "The sun is shining, the company is sublime," he said with a wink, "and there is nothing more to fear."

Abigail stopped and turned to face him. Her eyes were bright and she looked well rested, losing the slightly glazed-over quality he had noticed since their reunion at Edgemont.

"Have I properly thanked you for all you have done for me?" she asked.

"I did no more than facilitate what you were always capable of, my dear," he answered honestly. "You have always been strong. I know you had to be, to survive your upbringing as you did. It was only a matter of time before you would have found a way to free yourself of your father with or without my assistance."

She cocked her head to the side, and Colin found her nearly irresistible. Would this longing for his own wife ever cease? He prayed it would not.

"Perhaps, although I do believe it was more enjoyable with you along." She began walking once more. "In fact, I find most things more enjoyable when you are around."

"As do I. And your company is not so tiresome, come to think of it." Predictably, Abigail elbowed him in the ribs.

"Your safety and happiness are my sole priorities," he said earnestly. He glanced back the way they had come. Seeing precisely what he was hoping for, he grinned, and looked at Abigail once more. "And to that end, I would like to present you with a gift."

Slowly he turned her by the arm until she could see Morley approaching, a bundle in his arms. Speaking into her ear, he spoke over her shoulder. "Eliza was reluctant to see him go, yet I believe she knew he belonged with you. He will watch over you when I cannot be present, and I shall know you are always protected."

Abigail's squeal of happiness as she took Rascal from Morley's arms was proof he had made the correct decision as to a belated betrothal present.

"I apologize for the lateness of it, I would have liked to present it to you before the wedding, however he was too young to travel until now."

Abigail stopped cooing over Rascal and gazed up at him. "This is perfect," she assured. "In my entire life I never imagined being so happy, so content, as I am right now, in this moment. I do believe that I shall never wish for more."

Colin felt very nearly the same, although there was one undertaking he looked forward to with great anticipation. As a peer of the realm, he was responsible for more than simply himself. He was duty bound to provide an heir, and with a saucy grin, he could think of no more worthy a pursuit.

Acknowledgements

I am amazed with the generosity of those around me. My family and friends who are so willing to read over my unfinished products and suggest ways for me to make the story better, or the writing stronger, or the characters more believable.

Writing Abigail and Colin's story stretched me as a writer because I had to bring characters from one book over to another and somehow manage to remain true to their individual personalities. I am so grateful to my critique group, beta readers, editor, and proofreader for helping me with this endeavor. I could not have done this without each of you.

Most of all, I am grateful to my husband, Stephen, for always being my sounding board and being the greatest brainstorming partner I could ever have. He puts up with more than any of you will ever know, and his ideas often find their ways into my stories. Without him, and his uplifting support, I would never have made it this far, and I cannot thank him enough.

About the Author

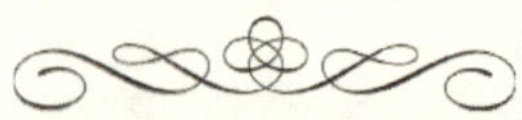

Kimberly Loper has had an intense love of reading ever since she could remember. As a child she would check out huge piles of books from her local library. She has loved the process of turning her ideas into stories to share with others. She has a bachelor's degree from Utah Valley University and currently resides in Utah with her husband and four children.

www.ingramcontent.com/pod-product-compliance
Lightning Source LLC
Chambersburg PA
CBHW031941240626
47153CB00003B/823

9781951908041